ESCAPE
THE O'BRIANS
BOOK ONE

JUDE MCLEAN

Edited by Paula Demary
Cover by Victoria Wright, www.PublishingWright.com

Published in the USA
ISBN: 9798508962340

Publisher: Jude McLean

www.judemclean.com

For Befy, Darcie wouldn't have a name, and I would be lost without you. And Bob, for giving me the courage to keep at it.

Thank you, my dear friends.

Sometimes fate has a plan of its own.

CHAPTER I

"FORGIVE ME!" she cried, as she knelt on the cold ground before the stone altar in prayer. But no answer came, and she was left alone with her guilt and grief for what was forever lost.

DARCIE HARTWELL WOKE UP, her tired face wet with tears. It was always the same dream. A small, empty church made of stone with no roof, high slated windows, and a hard gravel floor. The place felt ancient. A large, solitary stone altar stood at the front of the single room, bearing carved images worn from time. Images she couldn't decipher, no matter how many times she tried, but something felt different about them. Each emanated a profane feeling when she would place her hand on a carving, tracing the lines with her fingertips.

Outside the solid, heavy door was a vast field. There were two graves whose names were lost to age and weather, and only a few tall trees sheltering the place. Distant, snowcapped mountains surrounded the fields, but the ground was green and lush. A flowing stream wended its way beside the church, and the air around her was clean, carrying only a tiny bite of chill. The place gave her a feeling of both sadness and joy that she did not understand.

Darcie had visited many churches over the years, but none of them matched the one in her dream. She wondered if she had made it up, but the place felt real. Whether it existed or not wasn't her concern. Why the same dream had come to her so often over the years was what worried Darcie. Even more so, now that the dream was more frequent and carried an overwhelming intensity. The contradicting feelings of sadness, guilt, regret, and fulfillment took over her senses. Everything felt so real, but didn't make any sense. What did it all mean?

"It means you're looking for a reason to escape your problems," she muttered to herself.

Frustrated, she dragged her hands down her tear-stained cheeks and got out of bed to wash her face. The cool washcloth was a small comfort. Her reflection in the mirror stared at her with dark circles and puffy, bloodshot eyes. She used to be pretty, or so she was told, with her creamy skin and large green eyes, and a handsome boy once said her mouth was made to be kissed.

Those days were long gone. She sighed, and knowing she would not get any more sleep, brushed her teeth, braided her long auburn hair, and wrapped it into a bun at the nape of her neck.

Darcie's mundane routine helped take her mind off her dreams, but it didn't help take her mind off the fact that she was miserable. If she was honest, she had regretted her decision as soon as she had made it, but it had been too late to change her mind.

No one forced her down the aisle. It was her choice to keep her promise. She did everything she was expected to do, never wavering in her duties. That's all they were to her now, duties. She went from day to day, week to week, struggling not to scream and run away, leaving everything behind.

She lugged her way into the kitchen. It was too early to start breakfast, so she made herself a cup of tea with milk and sugar and stood by the sink, looking out the window. She watched the sun rising over the trees across the field and said a little prayer out loud, asking for peace and guidance.

"Peace of mind is a choice, not a gift."

Darcie jumped, spilling her tea.

Frances laid a hand on her arm. "I'm sorry, dear, I didn't mean to startle you. Let me clean this up. You boil us some more water."

"I was miles away."

"I heard. Come and sit with me." Frances finished wiping up the spilled tea and poured herself and Darcie a fresh cup. "I am going to come out and ask you straight. What is wrong? You have not been yourself for a long time now, and it worries me gravely. You hardly eat. I hear you up at night crying or worse, screaming in your sleep. I thought you needed some time and space, but now I wonder if I should have approached you sooner. I watch you go through your days as if you are in a trance."

Darcie opened her mouth to apologize, but Frances held up her hand. "Yes, you get everything done. Everyone is taken care of, but there is no joy, no spirit in your eyes. I know your birthday is coming up, and that always brings up the pain of losing your father, but I am genuinely concerned for you." She laid her hand on Darcie's, giving it a comforting squeeze. "If I can help, please allow me to do so."

Darcie looked into the empathetic face across the table and let out a breath. "The thing is ... " She hesitated. "I can't breathe here anymore, mother. I'm trapped in a life that no longer makes sense to me, and no matter what I do, this feeling of suffocation keeps clenching my chest." She balled her fist tight. "I know how selfish this sounds. You've taken care of me and kept me safe, and that makes me feel even worse." Darcie could no longer look her mother in the eye. She couldn't bear to see the inevitable disappointment.

Frances waited, choosing her words carefully. She placed her teacup down. "Darcie, listen to me. You can either disappear into this life, or you can dominate it. Only you can decide which is best. But for your own sake, I would suggest you decide sooner rather than later."

With that, Frances patted Darcie's hand and got up, taking her tea into another room as the others began parading into the kitchen for breakfast.

Darcie had the kitchen well organized, and breakfast went like clockwork. No one asked questions or commented. The mornings were always quiet. Darcie was grateful for that small grace.

After everyone had finished, she cleaned up and went on her usual morning walk through the field. The crisp morning air helped to clear her mind. She breathed in deeply and began to think about her mother's words. She didn't want to disappear, and she didn't want to dominate either. She didn't even care if she was happy, so long as she felt peace.

She used to be confident. Okay, maybe not, but she wasn't the scared mouse she is now. She had been happy, carefree.

Those days were so far gone she could barely see them anymore. *It has taken a decade for you to realize your mistake. That proves how inept and pathetic you are. You aren't capable of making the right decisions, not anymore.* She plucked a wild daisy and twirled it between her fingers as she thought. *Happy or not, it's best to stay put. At least here I'm safe.*

She looked over the field toward the morning sun. It was a view that had once brought her comfort. Now she couldn't help but feel absolutely nothing. With a sigh of resentment, she turned back for the house.

When she stepped inside the front gate, she froze. The sound of the iron gate closing behind her vibrated through her head. It was the door to a prison cell slamming her in. Suddenly, her lungs strained. The need to break free was excruciating.

CHAPTER 2

CONNOR O'BRIAN STOOD up and wiped his brow with his forearm. He looked around at his construction crew as he rolled his shoulders and circled his neck, easing his muscles. The sounds of the job were music to his ears, giving him a feeling of satisfaction. Doing something useful and important. That was what mattered to him.

He didn't notice the multiple women, much to the envy of his crew, who passed by trying to get his attention. He is through looking for his dream girl with the sea-green eyes. He has looked for years and never found her. His workers wonder if it's ambivalence or obliviousness. Whatever the reason, he's no time for women doing cartwheels, bending over backward, flirting.

Connor glanced at his watch. He had to get to the second job site to inspect the hotel remodels before a meeting with another client.

Leaning against his black SUV door, changing his dirty work boots, he wished he had given the meeting to his office manager. He much preferred to be on the site working with his hands than pushing a pencil and dealing with a bunch of stuffed shirts.

Since he was sixteen, Connor had worked, taking any job he could get in the construction business. Since then, he had started his own company. He was by all accounts a success, but only in business.

His personal life was another matter. He'd been engaged to his college sweetheart, who was with him through all his long workdays and schooling. He wanted to be a man she would be proud to call husband. When they started to plan their wedding, he bought some land near the local cliffs. It was his surprise wedding gift, and he couldn't wait to give it to her.

Connor arrived at her house and found it dark. He went inside using the key under the flowerpot. The flower was dead. The house was cold. She wasn't home, and it looked as if she hadn't been for a while. On the kitchen table was a note with his name on it.

He blew out a breath and unfolded the paper. "Forgive me," was all it said.

That was five years ago, and he still wanted nothing to do with women, except for the one who haunted his dreams. If she ever showed up, he would drop everything and chase her to the ends of the earth.

He was safe making that promise. The odds of her being real were slim to none. He didn't know who she was. He would reach for her, talk to her, but she never spoke, and all he saw were the striking, large sea-green eyes centered in the softest, lovely, haunted face.

The dreams had become more frequent. The feeling of her desperation and panic made his sleep uneasy. He always woke with a feeling that something was coming. He did not know the sound of her voice, but he knew the sound of her heart, and it was broken.

After the break-up, Connor had thrown himself into his work. He was able to give stable employment to a large number of employees. That's what mattered to him. A green-eyed woman would be a distraction. He had employees with families who depended on him, and he had no intention of letting them down.

They didn't deserve to be as unhappy as he was. Not that he would admit to anyone that he was anything but content.

He was a confirmed bachelor—whether he liked it or not.

CHAPTER 3

DARCIE STEPPED outside the Shannon airport, and when her foot hit the ground, the weight in her chest dropped into her feet like an anchor with a resounding thud.

She exhaled the nervous breath she'd been holding since jumping into the taxi and instructing the driver to take her to the airport. The sun was beginning to rise. Facing its brilliant light, she breathed in deep, absorbing its warmth. She knew she had done the right thing.

Only yesterday, she'd been watching the sunrise through her kitchen window. After the panic attack, she knew what she needed to do. She quickly packed a bag and slipped out the back door.

Darcie could hardly remember how she got here. It was like being in a trance. She had walked into the Boston airport with no plan. She bought a ticket and the next thing she knew; she was here. She didn't know why and didn't even care. It all felt right. She hadn't been so sure of anything in her entire life.

Her heart skipped a beat. Now that she was on Irish soil, she could breathe again.

She didn't have a care in the world—except to keep to the left side of the road. She was concentrating on staying tight to the middle line and staying on the left. Surprisingly, she wasn't white-knuckled on the steering wheel. But then she realized she was only driving thirty miles per hour on the highway. She was going to have to pick it up.

As she drove to the hotel, she couldn't help but pull over now and then. The landscape was so compelling. Everything was vast and green. Farms and castle ruins stood side by side. Hills soon became mountains and in the distance were small, colorful villages.

As she turned into the entrance of The Swan Lake Hotel driveway, she smiled. The gates were tall, Gothic black iron, and they were kept permanently open.

There were enormous moss-covered boulders that bordered the long winding driveway, and a few deer were grazing among them. Tall, ancient trees shaded the drive. She wondered what stories the rocks and trees could tell. There was history here, ancient history and magic. Not real magic, of course, but there was no denying that Ireland held something special. It pulsed through her blood.

There was once a time in Darcie's life when she had been outgoing, fun, smart, happy, more or less. That time was a ghost to her now. She was a ghost of herself. She thought she'd been defeated, but something inside her, within, was fighting to be free, to exist, to live. She had been hiding long enough.

Either disappear into this life or dominate it, mother had said. I don't want to disappear.

Darcie parked her blue Mercedes and took in the view. Yes, there was some magic in the air whispering, "Welcome home, my child."

She did a little dance, squealing with excitement, and with her head held high and the sun shining on her like a spotlight, she walked inside and tripped inside the doorway. *So much for a dignified entrance to my new life!*

And because she chose the new life, she decided to allow the laughter that bubbled up to have a voice.

CHAPTER 4

CONNOR HAD a contract with The Swan Lake Hotel to remodel an entire wing and was inspecting the progress. Each room would have all new layouts built. His crew wasn't due in for another hour so that he could check everything without any disturbance. The job was nearly finished and ahead of schedule, which pleased him.

He was standing by a window making a note when a bright streak of red caught his eye. It was a local woman whose long auburn hair burned like fire in the morning sunlight. She was dancing beside her blue Mercedes and laughing with a genuine smile. She seemed so free, so happy. He was envious of this woman and couldn't help but smile. He watched her until she was out of sight and shook his head, returning to his work.

DARCIE APPROACHED the hotel's golden front door and nearly fell face flat to the floor when they were opened for her just as she reached for the knob herself. She laughed; the man who opened the door laughed as well.

"I thought you were a goner, lass! Are you alright?" He caught her in his arms mid-fall.

She looked up into the welcoming face of an older gentleman whose light blue eyes gleamed. He wasn't laughing at her. He was laughing with her as he helped her stand.

"That's the best entrance to the hotel I've seen in some time. My name is Shamus, and if you need anything while you're here, you can call on me, lass."

"Thank you, Shamus. You might regret that after I harangue you with questions."

"You're an American then?" He sounded surprised.

"Yes."

"I wouldn't have guessed it for the world. Well, you will fit right in here. I can tell."

Darcie beamed at the compliment. She hadn't fit in anywhere in a very long time.

As she walked toward the desk, she took in the lavish decor. A vaulted ceiling with crystal chandeliers and intricate molding all around, it was all dark wood, kept in pristine condition.

Placed on antique side tables around the room were four large yet tasteful flower arrangements. The front desk was twenty feet long, and adorned with the same molding as the walls, and the carpet was a perfect shade of red with a large gold damask pattern.

Everything boasted opulence, but was welcoming. The place was an indulgence, to be sure, but she hadn't treated herself to anything in ages.

She got to her room and admired purple, burgundy, and soft gray furnishings, then stepped onto her private balcony that overlooked the lake. The view was spectacular. The mountains towered high above on three sides and created the feeling of having her own corner of the world.

On the lake were swans gracefully swimming past, as if they had no care in the world. On the far shore was the ruin of a castle. Small now, but she could picture how mighty it must have looked in its day. She would have to check that out. She stood outside, taking in the sunshine for a few minutes before stepping back inside. There was more about the hotel she wanted to explore. The girl at the desk told her about their spa. And that was calling her name loud and clear.

She glanced at the hotel map then decided it would be more fun to explore and find the spa on her own. How hard could it be?

———

FORTY MINUTES LATER, Darcie was lost. No signs, no people. She really should have brought that map along. The hotel was more extensive than she thought. She opened a door and stepped into a vacant hallway.

Connor was kneeling on the floor, winding an extension cord, when he heard a door open at the end of the hallway. He looked up and saw a woman he recognized as the one dancing in the parking lot. He smiled despite himself as he watched her decide which way to turn. She was lost. He was about to call out to offer help when she turned in his direction, making her way up the hall.

She hadn't seen him, but he certainly noticed her. Drawn to her large eyes, he nearly fell over. Time stopped. How did he not know before?

His throat constricted as he gulped. The face he would have known anywhere, the one he had searched so long for, was here in front of him. She was real and within his reach.

He tried to stay calm as his mind reeled. He stared, wondering if she would know him, and if she didn't, then what? His heart drummed in his ears as his eyes willed her to see him, know him. He wanted to run and scoop her into his arms.

He stayed still and waited.

Not in any hurry, she started up the hallway, looking at the pictures on the walls of Irish family trees, coats of arms, and paintings of the lake. Since the real lake was much better than a painting, she didn't pay much attention.

She passed a window and saw her car. At least now she had an idea of where she was.

Then she noticed him and froze. His blue eyes were so bright she could have seen them in the dark.

She was hypnotized and couldn't help but be curious. She continued to walk, forgetting she was lost. Her heart skipped a beat, then pounded in her ears as she approached. Her eyes round and unblinking, she didn't break eye contact.

Her lips parted for more air as she stole a glance with every step. He was holding an extension cord. He had a toolbox. He had dark hair. And a chiseled jawline. A well-kept short beard. And ... he was definitely staring at her.

Connor's eyes locked with Darcie's.

Something about him was drawing her in. She looked

15

again at the cord he held and hesitated. He put it down. She started to pulse as he stood up and smiled. His black T-shirt clung to his chest, molding to his lean muscles, and his jeans fit in all the right places. Heat rose through her body. She tried to steady herself and look away, but there was no refusing his beckoning eyes.

"Hello love." His smile met his eyes, his velvet brogue voice dripped like honey.

Her knees went weak, and she tripped over her own two feet. He caught her before she hit the floor. She looked up, expecting to see disappointment. Instead, she saw kindness in his eyes. A sense of calm echoed through her.

"You alright?"

"I'm sorry."

"No need to apologize." He held on to her a little too long, staring, hoping she knew him.

"I guess falling is a habit with me today. I tripped coming in the front door."

He had to restrain himself from caressing her cheek. Who caused such dark circles under her eyes? Who scared her? Made her run? He brushed her hair away from her forehead, then had to let her go before he went too far and frightened the life out of her. He stood her up.

"Thank you," she said. She could feel the blush flood her cheek.

Connor crossed his arms over his chest. "You're American?" That was a surprise. He tried to size her up but came up with nothing except that he needed to know more about this blushing American who haunted his dreams, danced like no one was watching, and somehow fit in like a local. "Are you lost?"

"What makes you think I'm lost?"

"This area is closed for renovations." He uncrossed his arms and softly smiled.

"I got lost trying to find the spa."

"Aye well, you'll find that downstairs. Keep going up this hallway to the end, where you'll see an elevator; if you go down two floors and to the right, you will find your spa. If you see a restaurant, you've gone the wrong way."

The longer he spoke, the harder her heart beat.

"Are you staying here?"

"Yes."

"With your family?"

"No ... I'm alone." She knew she shouldn't have told him, but he felt familiar. She was compelled to tell him anything he wanted to know.

She wasn't wearing a wedding ring, and her cheeks were still flush. He leaned closer. "I could walk you there myself."

Okay! She didn't want to come off as too eager, even though she could feel her eyes betraying her. "I think I can find it now. Thank you."

"That's a shame. I was hoping you would join me for a cup of tea."

"So, you weren't going to take me to the spa?"

Connor looked at the floor a moment with his hands shoved in his pockets. "I would have taken you there—afterward. I was hoping that while on our walk, I could tempt you."

She contemplated the consequences of saying yes. He was overwhelming all her senses. *Get a grip!* She needed to get away and clear her head. But she didn't have the strength to stay away from him. "How about a drink tomorrow? Only, I just got here, and I'm kind of tired from the trip." *That's sensible. Right?*

He let out a breath. "And for a moment there, I thought you would turn me down and break my heart. I'll meet you in the pub downstairs at half-six?"

"Alright." She nearly answered before he finished.

He couldn't resist taking her hand and bringing it to his lips.

She nearly lost herself.

"See you tomorrow."

His thumb caressed her palm as he slowly released her hand, making her breath seize. One more minute of his honey voice and dancing eyes, and she was going to faint into his arms.

"Bye."

He took in the view as she hurried away. *So that's what the rest of you looks like.* The woman didn't know him. But she would.

Thoughts of all the things he would like to do with her curves distracted his mind, and he tripped over his toolbox. *Shite.* Snapping himself out of his fantasy, he realized that he never got her name.

Buzzing with nerves, Darcie ran straight for her room and nearly collapsed against the inside of the door. She leaned back, panting with her eyes closed, replaying the encounter. The deep-rooted feelings seared her to her toes.

She touched her face. Her cheeks were hot. She needed to calm down. She jumped into the shower and let the hot water rain down. It helped her nerves relax. Water always did that for her. She got her sponge slathered with soap, and as she lightly scrubbed herself down, she could feel every inch of her body turn electric. She felt his eyes burning into her, and she shivered with anticipation as her thoughts turned to all the things she wanted to do with—*I never got his name!*

Darcie decided it best to forgo the spa. She was afraid of running into her Irish mystery man and losing herself in one fell swoop. She laid in bed thinking about him. She had never been so attracted to a man in her entire life. Her skin started to heat just thinking about him. But jet lag was creeping in, and she soon fell asleep.

CHAPTER 5

WHEN DARCIE WOKE UP, it was still daytime. She started to think about where she would like to visit. It was only a short drive into town, and she had some shopping to do.

She browsed in all the little shops while she daydreamed of what the next day would bring, having to control herself from whirling with excitement. She admired how each street had its own personality.

One lane was a brilliant display of bohemian color, with each storefront painted a different bright color. The next street over was posh, and the storefronts were elegant colors trimmed with black and gold.

There were two towering churches, one on either side of town, one Catholic, the other Protestant. She visited both and was in awe. They had outdone themselves. She knew that it had been illegal to be Protestant in Ireland. She surmised that once they no longer had to hide, they decided to give the Catholics a run for their money and built up a magnificent church to say, "We're here and not going away." If she was right, then they had definitely succeeded.

"Hello, how can I help?" A woman asked as Darcie walked through the front door of a charming boutique.

She looked to be about Darcie's age, was tall and slim, with golden hair that was cut very chic. Her makeup was minimal, and she wore flowing silk. To Darcie, this woman looked to be a free spirit and completely comfortable in her own skin.

"I saw a dress in your window—"

"I know just the one. I'll get your size. You go on back into the dressing room, and I'll bring it to you."

Darcie got a little flustered, but didn't have the heart to argue.

"Here you are. If you need help, give a shout."

Impressively, the saleswoman had brought the correct dress and in the right size. Darcie turned, looking at herself in the mirror. She stood silent, barely recognizing her reflection. She looked pretty. She wasn't used to looking pretty.

"You're quiet in there, you alright?"

"I just, well, I don't know." Darcie stepped out from the dressing room, and the saleswoman crooned.

"That dress has been waiting for you!" It was long and flowed to her ankle without dragging on the floor.

"Do you think so? I don't really wear things like this."

"You should start. This drapes perfectly, and that sweetheart neckline is showing off what you've got just enough." She noticed Darcie blush. "It's still modest, but with a little edge, and this shade of green makes your eyes dazzle. I don't know who you're going to wear this for, but I feel sorry for him. He won't be able to resist you!"

"I have a date tomorrow night. It's the first date I've had in a long time."

The woman squeezed Darcie's shoulders. "We've all been there. You get stuck in a rut, and before you know it, there are cobwebs in your hair—and other places, too." She winked. "And I have the perfect shoes." She handed Darcie a pair of flat, silver sandals. "Just a hint of sparkle to top off the look, Cinderella."

Darcie looked at the pretty sandals as if they would bite her.

The saleswoman recognized Darcie wasn't comfortable in her skin. "You know what you need? Underwear."

"Underwear?"

"I mean real underwear. You don't see in yourself what I see. You need to own what you've got and let this dress do the rest. And the best way to start is with pretty underwear. If you feel sexy underneath, then it will all come together."

She disappeared into another corner of the shop, returning with a matching bra and underwear made of delicate blue-gray lace.

"This is just what you need. It doesn't scream 'come and get me.' It's just beautiful, sexy, and elegant, just like you in this dress. Trust me. I've been doing this for twenty years."

Darcie laughed. "You're a very persuasive saleswoman."

"I wouldn't sell it to you if I didn't know you needed it."

She took a deep breath with one last look in the mirror. "I'll take it."

While Darcie was getting dressed, the woman called out to her. "This isn't just my job, you know? I own this shop. I can tell a woman's size the moment I look at her, and I can tell when she needs a little confidence boost. Women rarely see themselves for who they are. You just need to come out of your shell a little bit."

Darcie stepped out of the dressing room, looking sheepish. "I'm Sondra."

"I'm sorry, Sondra. I didn't mean to insult you." She looked away and began to wring her hands.

Sondra approached her with an honest, bright smile and took her hands, giving them a firm squeeze to grab her attention.

"Nothing to be sorry for. I wasn't correcting you. I was just continuing our conversation." She shrugged her shoulders and scrunched her mouth to the side. "Not many women talk to me. I'm successful, single and, let's face it, I have more fun in a week than most have in a decade. They're jealous. At least that's what I tell myself."

Darcie couldn't help but like Sondra. In a matter of minutes, she had exhumed a piece of Darcie that was long forgotten. She straightened her back and brushed her hair away from her face, holding out her hand in greeting. Her hand was warmly accepted, making them instant friends.

"As I said, I feel sorry for the man who has to be with you while you're wearing this dress. You're beautiful, and you've got the curves to make a man beg."

"Really? I've always felt like the big girl. I wanted to look like you."

"If we all looked the same, the world be one dull dinner party. Besides, I have no curves and would kill for some of yours. That makes us even." The two broke into laughter. Sondra rested her elbows on the desk and propped her chin in her hand. "So, tell me more about this date."

Girl talk. Darcie hadn't done girl talk in ages. "I just met him. He's well ... he's dreamy!" she swooned. "I don't really know him. I don't even know his name! But when he asked me out, I couldn't say no. He has a stare that burns right through me, a voice like honey, and I nearly collapsed when he kissed my hand."

"Oooh, you've got it bad! He sounds yummy."

"I'm nervous and completely out of practice."

"Relax and just be yourself. You'll be fine. I can feel it. And let's hope you get some practice!" Sondra bagged up the dress. "You know how they say it's like riding a bike? It's so much better than that! If I'm right, and I always am about these things, you'll be practicing before the night is over."

Darcie blushed again. Sondra found it charming.

"Come back and dish all the details. I haven't had an American friend before. It's time I had one."

"I haven't had many real friends at all."

Sondra couldn't imagine anyone not liking Darcie. "You have one now. Don't forget to shave your legs! And don't forget to come back for some girl talk. I want all the juicy details about Mr. Dreamy Eyes." She fluttered her lashes and pursed her lips.

Darcie laughed. "I promise I will."

CHAPTER 6

THE NEXT MORNING, Darcie was exhausted. Jet lag and a night's sleep that was repeatedly interrupted by a sexy Irishman would do that to a woman. She was a little cranky, but she got excited as she started to think about her date.

Her breakfast arrived, and she sat on her balcony basking in luxury and the warm anticipation of what was to come while she enjoyed the view of the lake and the ruins of the medieval castle. Black and white swans dabbled across the lake. It was peaceful, sunny, and perfect.

After breakfast, she went to find the spa. They had a hot tub with her name on it. Maybe she would get a manicure too. She hadn't done that in years. She looked down at her hands, at the bitten-down fingernails and decided against it.

As she ventured out, she remembered the directions her Irishman, she giggled at that, gave her, and she set her course, determined not to get lost when she turned a corner and crashed into a body.

Before looking up, she apologized. "I'm so sorry! Are

you alright?" She froze when his blue eyes narrowed on her. Her throat went dry, and her legs wobbled, causing her to stumble into his arms.

"We meet again. So eager to see me you can't wait until tonight?" he teased.

"I was ... " She was stammering.

"Looking for the spa?" He chuckled again, enjoying the effect he had on her. He held on to her as much for his pleasure as to keep her from slumping onto the carpet.

"Yes."

"I won't keep you from your pampering. By the way, what's your name?"

"Darcie. Darcie Hartwell."

"Well, Darcie Hartwell, I'm Connor O'Brian. Pleasure to meet you." He released her from his arms and kissed her hand. He looked from her hand through his lashes into her eyes with a devilish grin. She was practically humming. "I'll see you tonight. And Darcie?"

"Yes?"

"You're headed the wrong way, love." He pointed in the opposite direction and winked.

He flashed a smile as he strolled away. She leaned against the wall. She looked him up and down and blew out a long, heavy breath. Connor O'Brian made her want to howl.

CHAPTER 7

CONNOR'S EYES followed Darcie walking through the doorway of the restaurant, scanning the room for him.

She fiddled with her hair a moment and smoothed her flowing dress. Her hair was still a little damp. It had been so long since she had worn it down that she forgot how long it took to dry. She left it down with her loose curls hanging down her back.

He wanted to lose his hands in those long auburn curls and find out what was underneath that pretty dress.

Her gaze finally found him.

He was lost in a trance when she smiled. He took a sip of his whiskey to ease the lump in his throat. Never had he felt such an attraction. Darcie was a siren, and he was more than happy to drown at her will.

His smile made her knees want to buckle. Good thing she wore flat shoes, or she would be on the floor in a clumsy pile. She made a mental note to thank Sondra.

She walked to the bar where he sat sipping his whiskey and admired how at ease he looked, but when she looked closer, she saw something else that made her shiver with anticipation.

His eyes were fixed on her. He looked like he was going to eat her up. Lust filled her belly. All she wanted to do was crawl onto his lap and find oblivion in his arms. She wondered if he could see through her, and if he did, would he still want her? She brushed the thought aside.

"Hello, love."

There they were, the two simple words that had seized her attention in the brogue, hypnotic voice that dragged her under.

"Hello."

"If you don't mind me saying, you look gorgeous."

She blushed as he pulled a seat out for her. "Thank you," she said, looking at the floor.

He sat beside her, admiring how she didn't know she was beautiful. She was shy and gracious.

"Would you like a drink before dinner?"

"Dinner?"

He was deliberately throwing her off.

She took a quick breath and composed herself. "Is that how it is? You ask a girl for a drink, then turn the tables on her?"

He patted her hand. "Yes."

She wasn't going to argue. Spending more time with Connor sounded wonderful and, for once, she was hungry. She ordered a whiskey, downed it one gulp, nearly choking on the flame she had just swallowed. Her eyes bulged. She held her fist up to her mouth and coughed out a tiny puff of smoke.

He watched with anxious eyes and circled his hand on

her back. When she looked at him and smiled, he made a proud chuckle.

"That's my Irish girl. Sure, you may be from America, but you're one of us," he said, raising his glass in a toast. "Welcome home, darling."

"I'm sorry I crashed into you. I was trying to remember the directions you gave me and wasn't paying attention."

"Think nothing of it." He flicked a hand. "I'm sorry I didn't get your name when we met. I didn't realize until after I watched you walk away."

"You watched me walk away?"

"Yes, and a fine view it was." He sipped his whiskey and gazed at her over the rim of his glass. She was blushing again. It aroused him to know she wasn't aware of how bewitching she was.

They only had eyes for each other as they made their way to the table, instead of looking at everyone else's plate as they passed.

He pulled a chair out for her and smelled her hair as she sat down, letting her scent fill him. Images of her sitting over him with that hair hanging down, tickling his chest filled his mind. He needed to get a hold of himself. One step at a time.

He sat across from her, and they stared at each other for a quiet minute. She grabbed the menu. His stare was making her thoughts go fuzzy, or was it the whiskey?

All she wanted to do was release one long, adoring sigh. Instead, she asked, "What's good here?"

"Couldn't say. I don't get out much," he confessed. "But I've known the chef for many a year now. We were friends growing up."

"Did you grow up here?"

"No, in Caherdaniel. It's a grand spot to live, not much there in ways of building a business though. After college, I worked a few years, then I wanted to go out on my own. Be my own boss. He recommended my company to this hotel a few years back. I have a construction business. After that, business has never been better. I owe him a lot."

"He sounds like a good friend to have. Do you like being the boss?"

He ran his fingers through his dark hair. "I'll be honest, some days it's the worst job in the world. One of my lads had an accident today. Broke his leg. I had him tested for alcohol. Not a drop in him. He'll be off the job awhile, but I assured him he'll receive full pay, and his job will be waiting for him."

She felt a tug on her heart for someone truly generous.

"I was that glad. I wasn't looking forward to letting him go. He has a family to support."

"There should be more people like you in this world."

"Lucky for me, there aren't, or else you might be out with one of them instead of me."

"Good evening to you. Can I get you both a drink?" The waitress asked, intruding on their moment.

"How about a bottle of wine?" Connor suggested before Darcie could order another whiskey. No need to have her Irish flooding back all in one night.

The waitress watched them, their easy way, the longing in their eyes, and secretly hoped that one day she would have someone to look at her just the same.

She returned to the kitchen with their order. "You should see the couple out there. The way he looks at her is intense. They didn't take their eyes off each other even when they ordered."

The head chef peeked out the round window in the kitchen door, curious to see who had his waitress looking moonstruck.

"And yourself? What do you do for work? Or are you a spoiled heiress?" Connor teased.

"I set up charity organizations and events."

"That's noble work, to be sure."

Darcie shrugged her shoulders. "I worked with everything from the food pantry, shelters for battered women, all sorts of events for churches and hospitals. You name it, I probably did it."

"Did you auction yourself for a date?"

"Leave it to you to guess the one thing I didn't do."

The waitress poured their wine and left the table. Connor clinked his glass to Darcie's and each took a sip, not taking their eyes off of one another.

"You're here alone. Not many would have the guts to do that. I'm impressed. How long are you staying?"

"I don't know. I didn't buy a round-trip ticket." *Because I ran away and don't want to look back.* "I didn't want to get here and realize I made a mistake."

"Do you think you made a mistake?"

He looked at her like he knew her and heard her thoughts. "No, something tells me I'm exactly where I'm meant to be. I was nervous on the plane, but the moment I stepped outside the airport, I got this feeling. I can't quite explain."

"I believe the word you're looking for is fate."

He said it so easily. Fate. Who believed in that? Connor

obviously. Sitting in front of her wasn't just a handsome man, but one who was kind and generous. A man who deserved better than what she could offer. It was time to end the fantasy before it went too far. She knew just the way.

"There's something you should know. My birthday is this week. My fortieth birthday." She looked down at her lap. "I'm sorry I wasted your evening. Thank you," she paused to swallow the lump in her throat, "for asking me out."

Darcie didn't understand why, but at that moment it felt like she was lopping off her right arm. She didn't want him to go, but she knew he must. It was safer this way, less complicated. Darcie wrung her hands as her insecurity bubbled to the surface. Connor laid his hands over hers, holding them steady. She looked up.

"Happy birthday," he said as he caressed her hands. "I'll be needing to get you a present."

"No, you—"

Deliberately cutting her off, he sat back. "I'm thirty-seven myself. I wouldn't have guessed you were forty. But I'm glad you're not thirty."

She didn't know what to make of him. "Why?"

"When you're thirty, you think you know everything. The truth is you know nothing. A few more years of living doesn't do any harm, and it seems to agree with you," he declared, appreciating what was in front of him.

Darcie blushed from her feet to her face.

"So, are we done talking about your age, or would you like to try and find another excuse to push me away?"

Her mouth dropped open.

"I'll take that as a no." Connor smiled and tipped his wine, toasting his victory.

She had tried pushing him away, he'd refused to budge. She didn't have it in her to try again.

Every care melted away as she felt herself slowly drown in his pool blue eyes. His smile was warm, his gaze intense, commanding her full attention, making her forget all else. She blinked when another voice rudely interrupted their moment.

"Who's this enchanting woman that's put such a smile on my friend's face?"

Connor shook hands with a man dressed in chef's clothing. "Darcie, this is Flynn himself."

Flynn shook her hand. "Pleasure to meet you. You staying here at the hotel?"

"Yes, I am."

"An American!" Flynn jabbed Connor in the ribs. "Found yourself a beautiful distraction from your boring life?"

Darcie looked away, her eyes worried. She brought her hands close to herself and clasped them so tight her knuckles turned white. Connor reached across the table, taking her balled-up hands, easing them apart to hold them, reassuring her, telling her to pay no mind to Flynn, who stood there saying who knows what. It didn't matter.

"You should've said you'd be here tonight. No matter, don't bother with the menu. I'll make you something special. And if this gob shite gives you any trouble, you come to me, lass." Flynn winked and returned to his kitchen.

Connor raised her hands to his lips and placed a firm kiss on each hand. All was right again.

"He seems like a character," she said. An attempt to let go of her anxiety.

"He's a good lad. But I just might punch him if he winks at you again."

Darcie's mouth dropped open, making Connor laugh.

"That's twice you've given me that look."

Flynn was true to his word, making them an exceptional meal. But when he served them an appetizer of dehydrated cauliflower served with a tiny, painfully perfect cube of jellied balsamic vinegar, she had to restrain herself from scrunching her face.

Connor whispered, "I'm not eating this." He was poking the jellied vinegar with his fork, making sure it wasn't going to come alive. "Any room in your handbag?"

She tried to cut her cauliflower in half, thinking the least she could do was taste it, but when it shot out from under her knife and hit the man sitting behind Connor in the back of the head, only missing Connor's face because he ducked, they burst into laughter.

CHAPTER 8

CONNOR WAS CHARMING, attentive, and sexy as could be. Darcie couldn't help but wonder why he was single and what he was doing with her. It seemed to her that any woman would beg to date him.

"Can I ask you a personal question?"

"Ask me anything. I'm an open book." He gestured with his arms out wide.

"Well ... " She hesitated. "Why did you ask me out? Why aren't you with someone? I mean, you're successful, charming, handsome."

Connor's face lit up with a smile, raising one eyebrow as he leaned forward. "You think I'm charming and handsome?"

"That's not the point."

Connor leaned back. "Alright, you got me. Everything I told you is a lie. I'm no businessman, my family disowned me, and I've no friends. I recently got out of prison for murder."

Darcie's eyes widened.

"It was the daughter of my neighbor." He waved his fork. "The little shite wouldn't stop trying to sell me Girl Guides biscuits. One day when she knocked on my door with her wagon full of those disgusting chocolate biscuits, I stuffed them all down her throat, choking her to death," he said with an unrepentant nod.

Darcie swatted his hand. "Now, seriously, I want to know."

"Aye," he sighed. "The truth is, I had a long-time girl-friend. We got together at college. After a few years, I had my own company and felt I could give her the life she deserved. So, I proposed. A few months later I went to her house to give her a wedding present only to find she had upped sticks and left. She never called, just left. I never saw her again. It was a week before our wedding."

Darcie could see the pain in his eyes, and her heart broke for him. She reached for his hand in sympathy as he looked off into the crowded restaurant a moment.

"I found out through Flynn she'd been seeing someone else. So, guess I'm not so great as you think I am." He was starting to sulk.

Darcie sat up straight. How could any woman have hurt him like that? It wasn't right. The thought irritated her.

"Her cheating says more about her character and less about yours. She sounds like a mean piece of work. It's not your fault. You trusted the woman who was going to marry you." Where had that come from? She couldn't believe she insulted someone like that. "I'm sorry, Connor. I had no right. You loved her, so there must have been some good in her."

His fingers caressed her hand. "No apology needed. You got her number, to be sure. Too bad I didn't know you back then. I wouldn't have made the mistake of proposing to her."

Darcie thought about taking her hand back, but she didn't want to, and Connor was in no rush to let it go.

"You've good intuition," he said.

"What makes you say that?"

"You say you came here on a whim, but it feels like you are meant to be here. I think you were meant to get lost in the hotel so you would find me. So really, you weren't lost at all."

"Fate, huh?"

"That's right. The sooner you accept it, the sooner you will know peace."

Peace. If you only knew what I've done to try and find it. "How about a compromise? I agree to keep my mind open if you agree to answer one important question: what's for dessert? I could murder a slice of chocolate cake."

Connor laughed out loud. He noticed that she was more relaxed and took the opportunity to ask more questions without giving anything away and risk scaring her off.

"I thought most women would choose a tropical paradise to celebrate their birthday."

Placing her forkful of chocolate cake down, "I saw Ireland on TV when I was little. It looked magical. My parents said I was drawn to it because I was Irish. I knew I was adopted. So, when they explained that my biological parents came from Ireland and that made me Irish too, I accepted it." She shrugged her shoulders.

"You were adopted? What age?"

"Only a few days old. My biological parents died in a car accident." She took another bite of cake while Connor remained quiet, hoping it would urge her to continue. "When I was five, I noticed all my friends looked like their parents. My parents were blondes. That's when they explained my adoption."

"Have you met any of your biological family?"

"No. Family isn't defined by blood. It's about love. I was never treated differently than any other child, except maybe spoiled more. I was daddy's little girl."

"Was?"

She picked up her fork of chocolate cake and took a nervous bite. He was teetering on sensitive territory. "He died six years ago."

"I'm sorry." Connor felt terrible for asking, but was happy she was opening up.

"It's alright. My father wasn't going to get better." She felt a lump in her throat and took another bite of cake when he urged her to continue. "His last words were asking me to let him go. He wanted me to take care of myself, he loved me and wanted me to be happy."

She got it out without breaking down. She was turning her fork between her fingers. *Please, stop asking me questions. I'm telling you too much.*

Connor took her fork so he could hold her hands. "And are you happy?"

He was staring into her eyes. She couldn't help pouring her heart out, even though she knew she should keep quiet.

"If I'm honest, I haven't known a day's happiness in years," she admitted. "He was the only man I've ever really loved. I'm not very good at living up to his wishes." She quietly wiped away a tear.

No more questions tonight. Connor wanted to cradle her and whisper comforting words in her ear. Darcie had changed from a woman he desired to a woman he adored.

"I don't know why I told you all that," she said, shaking her head as if coming out of a trance.

"Because I asked." He weaved their fingers together. "So, you've never been in love?"

Embarrassed, she shook her head no.

"Maybe you will find love here," he said softly.

Darcie looked at Connor through misty eyes and smiled. "I'm surprised you didn't give me another speech about fate."

"Now that you mention it—"

"Don't."

"Why not?"

"Fate means that nothing is in our control. That everything, good and bad, is going to happen no matter what."

"I think fate is what you're meant for. It's up to you to choose whether or not to accept it. Bad things happen, same as good. They're what make you who you are, but they don't define you. Take your adoption. You could have decided they were just kind people who took in a helpless babe. Instead, you chose to see past that. They were kind to adopt you. They loved you and raised you as their own. And you recognized that family isn't about blood, it's about love. See?"

She had had enough talk about fate for one night and wanted to change the subject. She looked around the restaurant. It was empty.

"Where did everyone go?"

"They close at half ten. It's eleven."

"That's impossible." The time had flown by.

"Not when you're with the one person you've been missing in life." He knew she felt it. She had to, and even though they had spent five hours together, he wasn't ready to let her out of his sight. "Take a walk with me?"

He pulled her chair out and leaned into her neck. Her skin tingled at the sound of his breathing nearby. She tilted her head into his breath, closing her eyes as her heart leaped.

CHAPTER 9

CONNOR LED DARCIE OUTSIDE, where the grounds were vast, empty, and dimly lit. They passed the flower garden down to the lake's shore, where ruins of the ancient castle stood. He kept their pace slow.

As they strolled, she looked over the water to where the moon hung between two mountain peaks. It's cool light reflected off the ripples, making the lake appear to be liquid silver.

Neither said a word. Darcie took in the night air as if it was her last breath. In front of them, the ruins stood high, emanating ancient beauty.

Connor was caressing her palm. She was going to jump out of her own skin. The heat from his hand was enough to make her quiver. Then, as if he heard her thoughts, he tugged her to his body and stopped, barely a breath away.

"I'm sorry. I didn't mean to grab you so hard."

"It's alright."

"Can I kiss you?" he asked in a desperate voice.

She nodded her head. It was all she could do with her air cemented in her lungs.

It was a kiss so desperately sweet. His fingertips caressed her neck as his hand slipped down to her collarbone. She didn't know what to do with her hands as they rested warily on his chest. He took her hands, lacing them around his neck, and she erupted. The jolt sent him reeling as she fisted his hair, making their kiss deeper and desperate. He locked her in a grasp that alone would have left her weak.

All thoughts left her mind. Her body flowed with liquid heat. He felt her go limp in his arms and broke away, afraid he'd come on too strong. Breathless, she fluttered her eyelids open. He was relieved when he saw a woman helpless in his arms and not afraid.

"I'm sorry. I had to kiss you before I burst."

"Don't stop," she said.

He smiled as he softly brushed her mouth. He slid his hands down and grasped the ends of her hair, curling it around his hand, and gently tipped her head back. Her need mirrored his own that he was fighting to control.

Not far away, he heard voices. They didn't need an audience.

He led her inside the dark ruins. The stone walls towered forty feet, even though most of the magnificent building had long since fallen into the lake, victim to time.

Stopping inside an alcove, he pulled her to him in a crushing kiss. She trailed her hands down his back, feeling his muscles ripple and tense. He backed her up against the cool stone, making her shudder with every caress.

The more his mouth devoured, the tighter the knot twisted, so low. Her unfamiliar, glorious aching was unbearable. Her jaw chattered as she bit back the urge to twine herself around him.

She didn't realize how hard her fingers dug into his sides as he moaned. She was losing control. Finally, with what breath she could spare, she gasped out, "My room."

And then he stopped. His hands that were tangled in her hair, now rested on her shoulders. His breath hot on her neck.

It was like trying to see through a steamed-up window pane. Which was worse? The beautiful ache of enjoying or the empty, unfulfilled desire?

"I want to be with you." His hands slid down her arms and clasped hers. He shook his head. "But I don't want you to regret your decision."

Darcie wasn't having it, and pushed him away. Her shove wasn't enough to move him. He reluctantly stepped back.

"I'm a grown woman. Not some young bimbo without a thought in her head!" He didn't get to tell her what she did and did not want. She hadn't wanted a man, didn't look for one. Then he dropped in and changed everything in the blink of an eye. If he thought she would be told how to feel or what to do, he was in for a surprise.

She stepped forward into a sliver of moonlight that streaked her face. Angry passion glared at him.

"Jesus, Darcie, how can I control myself when you look at me like that?" She was the sexiest creature he'd ever seen when she was in a temper.

Without thought or warning, he pressed her hard against the wall. His assault of her mouth was fierce as he dipped his warm tongue in and out.

She felt him hard against her thigh as he dragged up her skirt. His hands found her most sensitive place and tore the lace away.

"Connor! If—"

"There now," he murmured.

She went liquid, collapsing inside his arms as he stroked her until she shook, then thrust his fingers inside her, moving in rhythm with his tongue, in and out.

Her breath was hard and fast while he feasted on her mouth. Dragging her under further and further. He took in her sound that mingled with his own until her cries escaped.

He watched her let out a blind, deep moan and strengthened his thrusts, making her cry out as she went off like a firecracker, shattering in his hand.

He pulled away and rested his forehead against hers as she panted and shuddered. She laid her palm over his chest, feeling his heart pound.

He held onto her. "Listen, I don't understand the hold you have on me, but I want to," he said, looking her in the eye. "I didn't want to take advantage of you. I shouldn't have even done what I did, but I just had to be inside you." He kissed her forehead and paused, catching his breath. "When you invite me to your bed again, I won't refuse you." Releasing a hot breath of submission, "I won't have the strength to say no to you again."

He stepped back to look into her eyes, worried about what he might find.

Darcie stared back for a long moment, making him sweat. "Connor... you owe me a new pair of underwear." She was only able to hold a straight face long enough to make her point before a little gush cracked her phony, stern expression.

He roared with laughter. "Fair enough." He kissed her solid on the mouth. "You're going to be full of surprises!"

━━━━━━━

As Connor drove home, he decided he had some wooing to do if he would convince Darcie they were meant for each other. He wanted to give her everything, be her everything. The thought of saying goodbye to her made his chest tighten.

Darcie sat on her balcony, savoring the night air and the view. The alcove they had been in faced her room. Her skin hummed. She ran her hands up and down her arms, thinking of what they had done. To be so intimate wasn't like her. But there was something special about Connor O'Brian. She trusted him absolutely. He stirred up feelings she hadn't ever had before. He said he didn't have the strength to say no, neither did she. Everything inside her had said yes the moment she laid eyes on him. Now that she had an idea of what saying yes would bring, she wondered how long she would have to wait to say it again.

CHAPTER 10

CONNOR WALKED through his office doors the next morning with a face like thunder. He'd hardly slept. When he did, all he saw was Darcie, only this time she wasn't silent. He heard her cries of passion and pleasure, smelled her, felt her, tasted her. The woman had hijacked all his thoughts and turned him into an idiot who put his shirt on backward. Luckily, he noticed that before he got to the office. And he'd nicked himself shaving.

He hadn't done that since he was a teenager who didn't have a clue what those few whiskers were really there for. They weren't there to make a boy look like a man, but to make a lady feel like a woman. And to make things worse now, he was forced to sit at his desk and do paperwork. He damn-well hated paperwork! *And if Nan gives me another one of her looks, I'm really going to lose it. Here she comes, right on time for me to tell her where to stick it! The nosy cow.*

"So, who is she?" Nan asked while she put a few papers in a filing cabinet.

"What? Who?" He went on to tell her she was a crazy,

46

old trout who needed to keep her own bleeding nose out of his bleeding business. And there was no woman.

"Connor Henry O'Brian, I turned you over my knee for lying when you were in short pants, and I will do it again!" She gathered up a few papers from his desk, turned to walk out, and then changed her mind. "Only two things give a man a face like yours, and the other one is a woman," she said as she gave the papers a little wave.

"If ever a man needed earplugs—"

"If ever a man needed a woman, it's you!"

Connor rolled his eyes.

"Call this number. He owes you a favor. Have him send her flowers right away this morning." She forcefully placed a piece of notepaper with a phone number on it in his hand. "Then you're going to call her and ask her to lunch."

He opened his mouth to protest when she held up a hand to his face.

"Take her someplace nice, but not so nice that she feels uncomfortable. Then, after you have enjoyed a good meal together, take her back to that gorgeous house of yours."

"Why would I do all this?"

Nan's tone softened. Her eyes showed pity. It pissed him off.

"Because lad, you love her." She turned and walked to her desk, leaving his office door open.

He picked up his cup of tea with a huff, shaking his head, and choked, nearly spitting out the vile liquid in his mouth.

Nan didn't bother looking up. "By the way, you picked up my cup of coffee. Your tea is sitting by the kettle. Eejit."

He stalked to the kettle to retrieve his tea and fixed Nan

a fresh cup of coffee. He would fire her if she weren't his godmother, and his aunt, and so damn good at her job that she was irreplaceable.

When he made his peace offering, she took it from him, took a sip, and said, "Lock the doors, ride her the rest of the afternoon and turn her inside out!"

Connor spat out his tea in shock.

"You'll feel better for it," she said, wiping the tea spittle from her cheek and nodding to his nicked cheek. "Both of you, by the looks of things."

As he left, Nan handed Connor a clean shirt and ordered him to take the next couple of days off, topping it off with a threat to hunting the woman down herself if he showed his face in the office. As he drove away, he smiled as he came up with an idea.

CHAPTER 11

DARCIE HOPPED in her car and drove in whatever direction she chose. Everywhere she went, the views were breathtaking. Mountains, fields, white-washed stone cottages, sheep, moss-covered stone walls tangled with wild fuchsia, winding dirt roads barely wider than a cow path. It was all new and yet somehow familiar. She had no idea where she was at the moment, but she was entirely at ease.

At a charming cafe, she enjoyed one of the best meals of her life. It was merely tomato soup, Irish brown bread with butter, and shepherd's pie. But it was all homemade, and nothing had ever tasted so satisfying. She asked the waitress if she could beg a recipe from the cook. Within a minute, a short, plump woman with curly gray hair came out of the kitchen, all smiles.

"I hear there's an American wanting my recipes!" she proudly boasted.

Darcie waved.

The woman studied her face, taking her chin in her hand. "You're no American. You're one of us!"

"My lineage is Irish, but I promise I'm American." Darcie chuckled with pride. It was nice to be accepted.

Flicking her hand in the air. "Ah! There you have it. You are one of us. I'm Grace, and this is my cafe."

"I'm Darcie, and I'm in love with your food! I ate every last bite, and I never finish a meal. That's the best meal I've had in years," she said sincerely.

Grace took Darcie by the arm, dragging her along beside her. "Anyone who compliments me like that can have any recipe they want. Come on in to the kitchen, lass."

The kitchen was small and tidy. A "cook's kitchen," Grace called it. Every last inch of space of the room was utilized. The walls had pots and utensils hanging on them, the ceiling too. The cupboards were wooden and old, with faded blue paint but sturdy; the appliances were nothing fancy.

But she didn't need fancy equipment. She was a natural cook. Everything smelled so good Darcie wanted to dip her finger into every pot. Grace chatted on, telling how the cafe had been started by her grandmother, for whom she was named, and then run by her mother and now herself.

"My granddaughter, Gracie, was your waitress. She's been learning to take over when I retire." Grace winked at her granddaughter through the doorway. "The day I retire is the day they carry me out in a pine box, so she shouldn't get too eager," she said as she stirred a pot of soup on the stove. "Do you have any family here?"

"Not that I know of. I'm adopted."

Grace turned to watch her while Darcie poked around the kitchen.

"I never knew my biological parents, and my adopted

parents were so good to me I never had any thought to finding what some call my real family."

Darcie shrugged her shoulders while looking through the pages of a cookbook. She had flipped to a page with a picture of a family sitting around a dining table and stood staring at it. Grace could see the scene upset her.

"Are your parents living?"

Darcie's bottom lip began to tremble. She placed the book back on the shelf and wiped her eye.

"You're too young to be without your parents." Grace laid a hand on her cheek. "But I can tell they did a fine job raising you. You'll see them again, and I'm sure they're proud as can be watching you from Heaven."

Before Darcie could explain, Grace continued. She couldn't hold back her tears as Grace petted her hair.

"You cry if you need to. Anyone who's lost parents as loving as yours has earned the right to a good cry." Grace gathered her into her chubby, comforting arms and let her pour her tears onto her shoulder as she cradled her, swaying.

"I never talk about them. Nobody ever asks." She lifted her head and sniffed. "Except Connor." She smiled and began to settle. "He wanted to know all about them and me."

"Who's Connor?" Grace asked, handing her a tissue.

"A guy I met. It's silly, really." Darcie wiped her face and took a breath, preparing to tell their story. "I ran into him in a hallway. Tripped into more like." She pictured their meeting. How his stare had drawn her in. What his hand felt like against her skin when he brushed the hair away from her face. He was a stranger, but he hadn't felt like a stranger at all.

Darcie's expression softened, and her eyes twinkled. "He asked me out right there on the spot. I barely know him, and yet I want to run into his arms, never leave and pour my heart out." She threw her arms in the air. "That's just crazy! Who falls in love in an instant?" She clapped her hand over her mouth. She had told herself it was all physical. It was safer that way.

Grace's face lit up. "Love at first sight? Bless my bride!" She sat Darcie down in a wooden chair beside the door and wiped her cheeks with the corner of her apron. "That's how it was with me and my Walter. I resisted, but he kept after me," she sighed. "I'm sorry now that I wasted time running away when I could have been spending that time with him. He died seven months ago. What I wouldn't give for another moment with him." She took Darcie's face in her hands. "Take it from an old woman who knows. If you love this man, don't waste time. Let him into your heart. You won't be sorry. Life is short. Spend it with the one you love rather than sitting around with regrets. Those don't keep you warm at night."

Grace wrote out her recipes for Darcie to keep under the condition that she visit again. That was a bargain Darcie was happy to make. Grace felt like an old friend. Darcie was finding that quality in a lot of people these days. Grace had given her a lot to think about. Connor wasn't the only one who believed in fate.

When Darcie found her way back into town, she saw Sondra's shop and decided she would stop in for more girl talk and shopping. Sondra was at the front desk when she heard the door open. When she spotted Darcie, she whooped in delight. There was no mistaking the difference. Her dark circles were all but gone, her eyes bright and her complexion rosy. She looked like a woman in love.

"If my eyes aren't deceiving me, I would say you got lucky with Mr. Dreamy Eyes!" Sondra whizzed by, flipping the shop sign to closed and throwing the latch. Then hurried to the small kitchen in the back to make tea, eager to hear about the big date. She placed a box of chocolates on the table. One can't have proper girl talk without chocolate. "Okay, spill it," she demanded, getting comfortable at the small round table with a chocolate in her hand.

Darcie opened her mouth to speak.

"Wait! Start from the beginning. And don't leave anything out!"

"First, Mr. Dreamy Eyes' name is Connor. I literally ran into him walking around a corner. It was so embarrassing. He caught me in his arms before I fell over."

"Oooo, this is going to be good. I like a man with quick reflexes."

Darcie giggled and went on to say she had been so flustered before their date she was afraid she'd put her dress on backward. "Thank you for the flat sandals."

When she got to detailing their conversation, Sondra stopped her. "This wouldn't be Connor O'Brian you're talking about?"

"Yes, you know him?"

"Not as such. He was remodeling a store nearby

recently. I saw him, and all I can say is that man is bleeding massive!" Sondra took a slow sip of tea, picturing him in her mind. "I tried everything to get his attention and got nowhere. He looked at me just once, straight in the eye, and never gave me another glance. He was searching for something. By the looks of things, I'd wager he was looking for you." She thought for a moment, studying Darcie. "He's one of the most successful businessmen in the county, you know?"

Darcie shook her head, wondering why he hadn't told her himself.

"I'm jealous! Tell me more!"

"He asked all sorts of questions and was genuinely interested. That was a little unnerving, but before I knew it, we had been there over four hours!"

Sondra stared at her with a scrunched-up face like she had eaten a sour candy that she forgot she hated. "Sounds like an interesting conversation. I can't sit through half a movie without getting distracted, and you're telling me this man sat over five hours talking with you?" She shook her head. "He's got it bad! Men don't talk, Darcie. Not like that." She put down her teacup, trying to fathom the character of Connor O'Brian. Deciding it was what it was, she looked at her eagerly for more. "I can tell we're getting to the juicy part."

Darcie's eyes went soft and dreamy. "He held my hand, and we walked by the lake. It was so romantic." She slowly exhaled. "He kissed me until I couldn't see straight."

Sondra cooed.

"He apologized for coming on so strong." She looked around the empty store making sure no one else was there to hear her confession. "I don't know what came over me. I practically jumped him."

Sondra leaned in closer. "And?"

"We went inside the castle."

"You got busy inside the ruins? We're going to need something stronger than tea!" She hurried to grab a bottle of whiskey and poured them both a drink. Sondra raised her glass in a quick toast and took a gulp. "Spill it!"

Darcie took a small sip of her drink, no need to have a replay of her impression of Puff the Magic Dragon, closed her eyes tight, and blurted, "He backed me up to a wall and nearly devoured me. His hands were everywhere. It was electric. Never in my life did I do this before, but I asked him to my room!"

Sondra's eyes got huge as she sat up straight in her seat.

"He said no."

Sondra slumped in her chair and flopped her chin on her fist. "You're holding out on me, I know it," she said, pouring them more whiskey. "We've all been there. I won't judge you."

Darcie threw back the entire contents of her glass. "He pulled my dress up and ripped my underwear off." She spilled as quick as she could in between coughs.

"You're definitely holding out! Did you have sex with him?"

Darcie felt the heat in her face and shook her head.

"Oh, I see. He got you off, but not himself."

Darcie nodded her head.

"That's hot!" Sondra raised her hands, marking each step of the story. "He turns you down, wanting to spare your honor, but at the same time can't keep his hands off you, and instead of bedding you right then and there, he pleasures you and walks away!" She fell back into her seat, fanning herself, breathing heavy. "So, how was it?"

Darcie's face was blistering just thinking about it.

"That good? If he can get you that hot with his hands, I wonder what he can do with the rest of his body."

"Sondra!"

"Come on! You can't tell me you haven't thought the same thing." Sondra let out a whistle of satisfaction, imagining the whole scene. "Aren't you a dark horse!" she cheered. "You're going to need some more underwear if he's going to just rip them off!"

Darcie laughed as Sondra hurried out of the kitchen, returning with an arm full of colorful lace and silk. "These ought to last you at least a week." The two broke into a fit of girlish laughter. "In all seriousness, it sounds like you and Connor really have something going here. I know it's been a long time for you, but my advice is to go for it. Life is too short for regrets. Something tells me you would regret not seeing this through."

After more conversation, whiskey, and a box of chocolates split between them, Darcie left with new confidence, a fully satisfied sweet tooth, and a slightly tipsy head. Talking with Grace and Sondra was just what she had needed. It helped her admit her feelings for Connor. The hard part would be putting those feelings into action. She still thought it was irrational, but she couldn't deny he made her feel more at ease and happy than she had been in years.

She passed a jewelry store on her walk back to the car and stopped to peek in the window. Off to the display's side was a gold necklace with a pendant of an intricate Celtic knot. One would nearly miss the two hearts in the center if they weren't looking closely. Whoever the artist was, they had taken great care in creating the piece. Something about it spoke to her. She was about to go inside the shop when she dropped a couple of shopping bags. Since she hadn't brought much of anything with her, Darcie had given herself a free pass to shop till she dropped—something she hadn't done in ages. After gathering up her bags and boxes, she got them balanced in her arms and decided it best to head straight to the car before she had another spill.

"GOOD DAY TO YOU, lass! Been shopping, I see. Did you have a nice day out?" Shamus asked as he opened the door for a barely visible Darcie. He peered around all the bags and boxes she carried to find her.

"Yes, I had a lovely day. Thank you!" She poked her head out to the side, beaming a smile at him, and headed for her room, declining the help he offered.

When she got in the elevator, she nearly lost her bags trying to press the button for her floor. She had just enough time to get herself together when the doors opened. She stepped out and dropped one of her bags again. With a huff, she bent down to pick it up, then fumbled with the others she thought she had balanced so expertly and ended up tripping herself right into a pair of arms.

"We have to stop meeting like this."

Darcie looked up into Connor's blue eyes filled with male mischief. "I was out shopping and dropped one bag, and then the others followed and—"

Her rambling was interrupted by his lips brushing hers as he pulled her in for a leisurely kiss. She tasted like whiskey and chocolate, and when he released her, she was dizzy. It took her a minute to get her bearings. He liked that.

That's better, now we're on more even turf. I have a miserable sleep, cut myself shaving, and get told off while she walks around fresh as a daisy drinking and shopping. Look at her dewy face and glittering eyes. She could at least have the consideration to not look so damn happy about it.

"So, what are you doing here? Another inspection?" She knew it wasn't that. "Thank you for the beautiful roses. I love them."

He would conveniently forget to tell Nan her idea of flowers was a success. "I came to see you," he said.

"How did you know what room I'm in?"

"Flynn looked it up after I threatened to punch him for winking and trying to seduce my woman away with his food."

"Your woman! Is that what I am?"

"I'd like to think so. You're not the type to go sneaking off into dark alcoves, driving a man half out of his mind with sex, but you did with me. So yes, you're my woman."

Darcie felt that same knot begin to tighten that she had the night before. Her heart began to race.

"You're blushing again, love. Do you always do that, or is it just around me? I'd like to find out." He leaned closer. "Too bad it was too dark for me to see if you were blushing last night when I had you in the palm of my hand."

"Shhh!" She clapped her hand over his mouth. "Are you crazy? Someone might hear you!"

"So, what if they did?" he chuckled. "I don't care. All I care about is when do I get to spend time with you again?"

His voice was smooth and seductive as he ran the back of his hand over her collarbone. She wanted to jump into his arms. *Get a grip!* "Well, I—"

"Are you free tomorrow?"

"Are you going to let me finish a sentence?" Straightening herself from her little tizzy. "Yes, I'm free tomorrow. What did you have in mind?"

"How about I take you on a day trip driving? You can sit and relax while you take in the sights."

"That sounds lovely. Wait, you aren't going to talk like a tour guide, are you?"

"I may have a story or two I could tell, but no official tour. Cross my heart."

When she asked where he would take her, he flashed a mischievous smile, insisting it was a surprise. Seeing she wasn't going to get an answer, she helped him collect her scattered bags and froze when he picked up a pair of purple lace underwear that had fallen onto the floor.

"I see that I don't need to buy you that underwear after all," he said, dangling them from one finger looking them over. "These are nice. I'll try not to rip them, but I make no promises."

She tried to take them away, but he held them out of her reach. When he placed the underwear back in the bag, he saw there were more. His eyebrows shot up with a grin.

"Women like to have pretty things. It's not always about men and sex!" she snapped, trying to keep her dignity as she snatched the bag from his hand.

"If you say so, darling. Can I say one thing?" She turned

to him, glaring. "My favorite color is red." Her face turned ten shades of red, and he burst into laughter. "Alright, I promise I'm done teasing. Let's get your bags to your room."

She turned on her heel and hurried away, leaving him to try and keep up.

———

"JUST LEAVE the bags on the table," she said as she waved her hand, dismissing him.

She stood with her arms crossed and one foot pointed, tapping the beats for him to leave. He placed the bags down and turned to face her. That miffed look was in her eye, and if he had learned anything about that look, it meant she did not want him to leave, which was good because he had no intention of going.

He crossed his arms and narrowed his bright gaze, putting her on notice. A thrill zipped up her spine, and despite herself, she cracked a smile as his mouth half curled. She couldn't resist that devilish grin. But on principal, she was going to try, sort of.

He stepped forward. "Are you so upset that you won't even invite me in for tea?"

"I could, but then I would have to invite you to dinner. Isn't that the way it works with you?"

"Touché."

"And I didn't ask you to carry my bags."

"Aye, but you can't tell me you wouldn't have scattered all that underwear after dropping the bags while looking for your key buried in your handbag." He took another step closer. "When you see it my way, I did you a favor."

Two could play his game. "Is that right? So, you think I'm clumsy and disorderly?" She threw up her arms. "You really know how to woo a woman."

"No, I don't think those things of you," he said softly. "But I've eyes in my head that tell me I make you flustered."

He had her number as he approached her like a cat sneaking up on its favorite toy. His expression spelled trouble, the kind she had thought of all morning. She could still feel his hands on her, inside her from last night. She couldn't help it.

Whatever it was between them couldn't be stopped. She trusted him. He made her feel secure, safe, and bolder than she had ever been on a day in her life. But she wasn't going to throw herself at him again. If he wanted her, he was going to have to come and get her. She stretched her arms out, holding him back.

"Connor, you stay there. You said yourself last night—"

"Last night is all I've been thinking about."

She stepped back as he eased closer. Nearly back to the balcony door, she looked for a way around him. "You're looking at me like I'm something to eat!"

He crooked his finger at her. She shook her head. He grinned when she allowed him to cage her against the door between his stretched arms.

She noticed the nick on his cheek. "Is that my fault?"

"It is," he said in a pathetic voice. "And I hit my head on the roof of the car and spilled hot tea all over myself."

"You did?"

"No, but if it will make you feel sorry me, I'll go out

and do that now." She gently touched the nick on his cheek. "I was distracted by the thought of a green-eyed woman kissing me." He leaned in to nip at her throat.

"Who's that at the door?"

He turned as she jumped onto the bed to get around him. "Trying to get me into bed again? I said tea. Not tea and me!"

She laughed, and he pounced. Squealing as he plucked her off the bed and played like she wanted to get away as he stood behind her, gripping her waist.

"Unless you're going to model those lacy things for me right now," his voice was thick, "I think a kiss is the least I should get for the torture you're putting me through."

"I'm torturing you? Who's teasing who right now?"

The heat in her belly went low. She could feel herself going limp in his arms as he brushed her hair away from her neck to nibble her ear, working his way down as his hold on her waist got tighter. She reached back and gripped his head as she moaned.

"Why don't you kiss me?" he asked as he splayed his hand just below her breast. She gave him a quick peck on the cheek. "I mean, kiss me the way you did last night. The kiss I can't stop thinking about."

He could feel her pulsing, and reacted quickly. He had to get her away from the bed before he took her right there and then. Spinning her around and hitching her up, her legs naturally wrapped around him as he braced her against the wall with his body, freeing his hands to roam.

But her soft mouth, and her warm skin, the delicate, tempting scent in her hair, her heavy sigh. It was too late. His ropes snapped.

She slanted her mouth over his, parting his lips. Her tongue delved deep, pushing him into a frenzy. He broke their kiss to catch his breath. Her face was flushed, her lips swollen. His breath ragged and hands greedy.

"I can't keep my hands off you. You're all I've thought about," he said, placing his hand flat on her cheek. "I know I promised to wait. I don't think I can keep that promise." He dove in for another passionate kiss. "Ask me again to your bed. I won't do it if you don't ask. I'll go if you want me to."

She couldn't bear it if he left, and she didn't have the strength or desire to tell him to go. Every sense screamed yes. She held his face in her hands and whispered, "Please, don't go."

Connor's heart gave a hard thud as the blood rushed in his ears. Her expression, her tone, her words held it all.

He wanted to enjoy everything about her, savor every sensation before desperation and heat blurred his senses.

He knew once he had her underneath him, there would be no stopping him. Hot and fast, it would be. He had wanted, yearned, longed for her too much, for too long to be tender. He had to give her this moment before it was all lost to blind greed. Did she say something?

"Connor, hurry."

He wanted more, needed more, and took it.

If he wasn't careful, he was going to leave her looking like a teenager who just stumbled out of the backseat of a car on prom night. He ran his hands down the side of her head, the back of her neck, down her shoulders, and cupped her breasts, teasing and feeling as he took a lace-covered nipple in between his teeth and lightly tugged.

She began to writhe and came hard when his fingers thrust inside her.

She went limp in his arms.

He carried her to the bed and eased her down as gently as he could, which was still two steps from tossing her around like a bag of cement.

Hovering, he caressed her face, looking deep into her eyes. One last look. She reached her arms out, inviting him, and he accepted.

They moaned into each other's mouths when he slipped inside her.

He held still a moment, shuddering at the feel of her. "I can't explain it. I wanted you the moment I saw you. I've never wanted anything so badly."

"I felt the same way." She bucked as his mouth found a sensitive spot behind her ear. "I swear this isn't like me. I've never—"

He caught her mouth with his, taking her under. There were no more words to say.

She nodded her head, and they began to move as one. Together, rising and falling, up and over.

She hugged him hard. He buried his face in her hair and held on as if she would disappear if he let go.

They lost themselves to each other as they rocked back and forth, back and forth. Moving as if they had been together in another life. Old lovers reunited.

Their breath heavy and their bodies trembling. He tucked her hair behind her ear and wiped the small tears that fell from her bright eyes, speaking Irish words she did not understand but felt their meaning. Now that I found you, I won't let you go. Acushla: my pulse, my darling.

What began as a feverish, unrehearsed game ended as a harmonious awakening.

———

THEY LAID in bed face to face, watching each other. She noticed something change in his eyes.

"What's wrong?" she asked.

"It's a bit late to be asking this now, but are you on the pill?"

She started to move away. He caught her waist, holding her steady. "I'm sorry," he said.

"No, it's not that." She met his eyes. "The thing is ... I can't have children," she said in a small voice. "I haven't been with anyone in a long time if you're worried about—"

"No." He stroked her cheek. "I haven't been with anyone either. I wasn't thinking clearly. I didn't plan on this, on you. So, I wasn't prepared."

She nodded her head, understanding, and let him pull her in for a cuddle. Entirely at ease, she draped her limbs over him, laid her cheek over his heart, and closed her eyes.

"Does it upset you that you can't bear children?" he asked as he combed his fingers through her long hair. A mindless gesture that she never knew she liked until now.

"It did at first. But I was adopted and had a wonderful life."

"You're a rare woman, Darcie."

"Do you want children?" she asked.

"If I had the right woman by my side, yes, I would." He tipped her chin with his fingertips. "By my blood or my name."

SHE WOKE up late in the evening, alone. On the bedside table was a note:

I HATE to leave you while you look so sweet sleeping, but there are a few things I have to do for our day out tomorrow. I miss you already.
Sweet dreams,
Connor
P.S Wear the purple underwear.

SHE ROLLED OVER IN BED, holding the note doing an excited bed dance. But soon, the only thing she could think of was dinner. She ordered room service and curled up in bed to watch TV.

When the knock sounded, she threw on a bathrobe and answered the door, expecting it to be her dinner, and was shocked when Connor burst through her doorway.

"I missed you," he murmured into her mouth.

"It's only been a couple of hours."

"It's been much longer than that."

Caught up in the moment, his meaningful words were lost to her. He didn't waste time. Before she knew it, they were in bed. She was lowering herself onto him when a knock sounded on the door.

Connor banged his head back against the headboard. He had waited years to be with her. Now who had the nerve to interrupt?

"I ordered room service." She covered her mouth, muffling her laughter. "You stay. I'll get the door."

She hesitated, suddenly very aware that she was completely naked. The bathrobe that was no more than five feet away may as well have been a mile. She stared at it. Since it wasn't going to levitate itself, she was going to have to get it. Connor watched with amusement.

"I saw you naked earlier, you know?"

She crossed her arms over her breasts. Nope. She couldn't do it. "Close your eyes," she said.

He refused to close his eyes and instead pinched her bottom, making her jump off of him.

With a glare, she hustled to her bathrobe and went to the door, turning around to make sure he was out of sight. "I can see your legs from here," she whispered. His legs disappeared, and she opened the door. "Flynn?"

"My waiters are busy, so I offered to bring your tray when I saw the order was for you. I couldn't have our favorite American waiting for her dinner." He began to step inside the door, but Darcie stopped him.

"Thank you. I can take that. I was looking for something in my bag, and everything ended up tossed all over the floor. I wouldn't want you to trip," she lied, trying to keep a straight face.

Flynn glanced at her feet and saw Connor's clothes in a pile. He smiled and wished her a good night as she closed the door. She put the tray down and broke into laughter.

"What's so funny?"

"Flynn saw your clothes. I guess that cat's out of the bag." She couldn't stop giggling. Darcie was officially a scandalous woman. She had never been that before and it tickled her to be one now.

LATE IN THE NIGHT, Connor woke to the sound of her crying and quickly turned on the lamp. She had rolled out of his arms and was sound asleep, but her face was wet with tears as her shoulders heaved. She said, "forgive me." Instinct told him to pull her in close. *Acushla, breathe with me.* Her crying stopped. He whispered Irish promises with a hope to chase away whatever was upsetting her. She never woke and slept the rest of the night quietly. *What made you run? Whatever it was, I'll keep you safe. We're together now.*

CHAPTER 12

DARCIE WOKE UP BESIDE CONNOR. His arm over her, she was glued to his solid, warm body. She caressed his arm while thinking about the days before. She couldn't remember the last time she was serene and happy. Being with him was easy and natural. She would work on not being self-conscious when naked in front of him. She exhaled, savoring the moment.

Wanting to brush her teeth, she tried to wiggle out of his embrace without waking him. She giggled when he latched onto her, rolling them over the bed.

When he gave her permission to brush her teeth, she took a pillow and politely socked him with it. He loved the playful side of her and was more than happy to indulge in instigating a pillow fight. By the time they had exhausted each other, the bed was in shambles, and pillows were scattered everywhere. They looked around the room, laughing at their handiwork.

She never did get to brush her teeth before he had to leave to get something for their day out.

She showered and dressed, choosing jeans, a white short-sleeved T-shirt, black Converse sneakers, and a navy-blue cardigan. She looked in the mirror and decided to put a light dusting of face powder on; her dark circles were all but gone, a swipe of blush and mascara, and a loose French braid with long, curling tendrils free around her face. With a last glance, she decided she was happy with how she looked and bounced downstairs.

"Good morning, Shamus!"

"And a good morning to you, lass! Where you off to today?"

"I don't know. It's a surprise. I'm going on a day trip."

"Aah, would that be with Connor O'Brian then?"

"Yes," she gushed.

"Well, I think you will find he is waiting for you just outside in a fancy car."

Shamus pulled the curtain back on the window. She jumped up and down, screeching like a teenager. Shamus chuckled as he opened the door for her. She turned and gave him a peck on the cheek before skipping outside.

He turned to see the hotel manager behind the front desk, looking on in amusement. Shamus shrugged his shoulders with a smile. "She's a right little dinger, that one!"

Parked at the curb was a teal-colored vintage Cadillac convertible with white leather seats that had a wide middle stripe matching the teal paint. Connor was leaning against the side. The sun was shining on the sparkling clean car and lit up auburn highlights in Connor's hair she hadn't noticed before.

"Where did you get this beauty?"

"There's a man I do business with that collects these. He let me borrow it. Like it?"

"I love it!"

He opened her door after kissing her good and long. She started to climb in when he stopped her. He leaned close to her ear, asking if she was wearing her purple underwear. She pulled up the band just enough from her waistline for him to peek at the lace. He growled into her hair and bent down to her exposed skin to steal a quick nip.

As the Cadillac pulled away, the curtain in the hotel window closed.

CONNOR STARTED to drive slowly out of the winding driveway when he reached for the glove box and pulled out a red satin gift box with a gold bow. She opened it up to find a green silk scarf.

"I thought you might like something for your hair, so it doesn't blow around with the top down."

"It's beautiful, thank you! You thought of everything, didn't you?" She kissed his cheek and proceeded to tie it around her face. When she put on her sunglasses, she felt like a glamorous 1950s woman.

As they turned out of the driveway, Connor flipped on the radio to an Oldies station. Elvis Presley came on singing I Can't Help Falling in Love. He couldn't have been more pleased with the coincidence of the song.

"How did you know I would like all this?" she asked.

"Over dinner, you mentioned that you and your

parents used to listen to Elvis and that you like the Oldies' songs. I took a chance with the car."

She didn't remember telling him that. A tear came to her eye. She turned to dab it away before he could see. He noticed and invited her to slide over and put her head on his shoulder. She was quiet until he turned the car onto the N70 toward the Ring of Kerry, then she got excited.

"Is that where we're going? I heard The Ring is one of the most beautiful places in Ireland."

"It is at that. You'll see—"

Her sudden screech cut him off. "This is one of my favorites!" She turned up the radio and swayed, singing along to Sh-Boom. "I haven't heard it in ages."

Life could be a dream if only all my precious plans would come true. If you would let me spend my whole life loving you. Life would be a dream, sweetheart.

Jesus, did he love seeing her happy and free like she had been while dancing in the parking lot. If he were honest with himself, he would say that he'd fallen in love with her that instant. He wanted to make her this happy for always, but knew that it would scare her away if he told her how he felt. Not everyone believed in fateful love at first sight. He didn't—until he saw her, and then everything changed.

As she watched the sun-kissed landscape go by, her mind began to buzz. Mountains and wavy green fields surrounded them. It reminded her of her dream. She hadn't given it any thought until now. Without explanation of the dream, she described the church. He confirmed there was one nearby. As Connor slowed the car to a stop, her heart pounded. This could be the one. She wasn't sure if it was excitement or terror she was feeling. She took his hand and made the walk across the field. It came into view.

An old stone church with empty windows and a large cemetery. It wasn't the one. She shoved it from her mind. She wasn't going to let disappointment ruin her day.

"Can we stop there?" she asked, pointing to a beach.

He pulled in and parked the car. She got out to admire the beach but was disappointed the waves were flowing up to the large rocks on the shore, covering all the sand.

"Something wrong?"

"I was hoping to walk on the beach." She looked over to see Connor taking off his shoes and rolling up his pant legs. "Isn't the water cold?"

"No, it will be grand."

She hurried to get her sneakers off and roll up her pants. They walked hand in hand down the path between the rocks to the water.

Darcie stepped into the water and shrieked. "It's freezing!"

He stood, laughing.

"You knew it would be this cold? I am so going to get you for this."

Connor howled with laughter as a cold wave splashed up her back. She was frozen, watching him sneak away. She went after him, splashing all the way as she chased him down and jumped into his arms. He caught her easily, but staying upright was another matter. She was wrestling to make him fall. He took hold of her braid and tugged her head back.

When he had her attention, he crushed her with a kiss,

making her forget about spilling him into the cool waves. He was drowning himself in her kisses when a wave splashed right up his backside.

"Haha! How does that feel?" she asked.

"I needed a cold shower." He slid her down his body, releasing her back into the water.

They walked along the beach for a while, but it wasn't long before Darcie's teeth started to chatter.

"Had enough for now?" he asked.

"It's so beautiful and peaceful here. I don't want to leave, but my feet are frozen."

He picked her up, carrying her back up the beach. She laid her head on his chest, listening to his heartbeat in one ear and the sea in the other.

"I've never seen a place like this before. It's dramatic and graceful. Even the air moves differently here." The mountains stood guard to the left and right as the ocean stretched wide in between. "It's like I stepped through a doorway into another world."

"Are you happy in this world?"

"Yes."

"Then stay." There. He'd said it. He cringed, waiting for her response.

"Maybe I will."

CONNOR PULLED towels from the trunk of the car to dry off their feet. "You had a towel?" she asked.

"Yes. And I have a pair of wellies for you, too." He held

up a pair of purple wellies that he was rather pleased with himself for finding. "I thought you would like a pair to match your underwear."

She couldn't help but laugh. "You knew I would want to go in the water? And you had wellies for me but didn't tell me?"

"It was more fun this way. How else would I have gotten you to jump into my arms?"

"That's a dirty trick. But you're right. It was fun!"

———

"THIS IS FANTASTIC! You grew up in Kerry, right?"

"Aye. Want to see where?"

"Yes."

"It's not much further. My parents are looking forward to meeting you."

She overlooked the fact that he had obviously made plans to take her to meet them without asking her first. "You told your parents about me?" Her eyes grew wide as she pulled down her sunglasses. "You don't have one of those relationships with your parents where you tell them everything, do you? They don't know about … ?"

"What?"

"You know … us … doing … stuff."

"Stuff? Like going to dinner, you mean? Or would you be referring to me tearing off your underwear and making you scream like a banshee in heat for all to hear?"

"Connor!" she shrieked.

"Aye, like that!"

She couldn't help but laugh.

"No, I don't tell my parents that stuff. I told them I met a nice lass, that we'd be driving down The Ring and would stop by, is all."

She began to fidget and checked herself in the mirror.

"Come here you. Just be yourself. You're lovely." He brought her under his arm and kissed her scarf-covered hair.

Her tension melted when he pressed her head onto his shoulder and told her a childhood story about fishing with his cousin Simon. His musical voice filled up her senses. She could smell the fish, and the sea, feel the boat's rocking, and see a small Connor holding his fishing pole.

She had forgotten about being nervous when he turned onto a narrow road and approached the most charming cottage she had seen yet.

The house was straight out of a picture. Stone walls painted white, a thatched roof, red window boxes with an array of flowers flowing from them, and a cheerful yellow door. It was opened by a woman who was no more than five feet tall, but if you asked her, she was a solid five foot two, plump with a fluffy bob of red hair that was just beginning to fade, and dazzling blue eyes that matched Connor's. She greeted them with a sweet smile.

"There's himself! Come, give me a hug." Her arms barely reached around Connor. "And this must be Darcie. Connor has told me all about you." She took Darcie's hands, giving them an assuring squeeze with her soft, chubby fingers.

"It's nice to meet you, Mrs. O'Brian."

"None of that formality here. Call me Sylvia. Come in, the pair of you. I've got lunch waiting." Sylvia ushered them inside. "Your father's out back and will be inside in a minute. Darcie, can I offer you a cup of tea?"

"Yes, please."

Sylvia passed Connor and winked with approval as he pulled a chair out for Darcie to sit.

The inside of the house was as inviting as the outside. Dark wooden floors, brightly painted walls of china-blue, potted plants scattered around, family pictures, and an impressive amount of artwork from around the world.

"You have a lovely home, Sylvia. It looks like you've done a lot of traveling?"

"Yes, Henry and I have been all over the world."

"Do you have a favorite place?"

"Well, I'll tell you." Sylvia laid a tray of tea down and sat across the table. "We've been to Africa, Egypt, Australia, and many more, including parts of America. I always love seeing the new places, meeting people, tasting the food, soaking in the local color, you know? But I love coming home. This is my favorite place. What do you think of Ireland so far?"

"I don't have the words. To say it's beautiful is inadequate. But something here speaks to me, and I just love it," she said with what she thought was too much enthusiasm. "I know. That sounds silly."

Before Darcie's hands had time to clamp together, Connor reached across her lap, taking them in his to calm her nerves as he leaned in close and murmured. "Acushla, nil se amaideach." Darcie's recovery was as swift as the dip.

Sylvia mused how Connor had always fixed things. He was always building things up, building something better. It was his life's work. Darcie was a natural fit for him. "Not at all. Ireland knows its own, and she welcomes them home with open arms. There's no doubt you're one of us, Darcie. So, it's your home that's speaking to you. Nothing silly about that."

Connor squeezed Darcie's hand as she beamed with pride.

CHAPTER 13

Sylvia saw something special about how her son treated Darcie. The streak of her insecurity that he washed away with one sentence and a tender gesture. And the way Darcie looked at him; unspoken words with her eyes that Connor understood. Sylvia had never heard him speak Irish to a girl, either. But it was more the way he said it. She knew of long marriages that didn't have an understanding like the one she was witnessing.

Sylvia looked away before the loving sight of her son with Darcie made her tear up. She casually dabbed her eyes and regained her composure.

"Aye, Syl'! Be sure to come get me when Connor and his American get here," Henry said.

"They're here now, you old fool."

"I'll only be a minute."

Molly, a red-haired Cairn terrier, announced their entrance and came charging into the room, aiming for Connor's lap, but was quickly enamored with the new guest and leaped onto Darcie's welcoming lap. Darcie couldn't have been more pleased.

"Looks like you've been replaced, Connor," said Sylvia as she watched Darcie play with Molly like they were old friends.

Henry came inside, brushing off his pant legs at the back door. He was a staunch man standing at six feet, with thick, dark brown hair, and a neatly kept beard that made his slate-blue eyes more prominent. He had muddy wellies on that he was in the process of pulling off when Sylvia scolded him for getting mud on the floor. He quietly placed them outside the back door.

"Sorry about that. I didn't see you drive in. I would have met you at the door. I'm Henry, and you must be Darcie."

"It's nice to meet you, Mr. O'Brian."

Henry reached to shake her hand. "Please, call me Henry. And I see you've met our Molly." Henry ruffled the shameless dog's belly that was laying upturned on Darcie's lap. He hugged Connor and sat down for tea. "So, Darcie, this your first time in Ireland?"

"Yes."

"And what do you think of our fine island?"

"I haven't seen much yet. But what I have takes my breath away."

"She was just saying that she hears it speaking to her," Sylvia said.

"Of course, she heard me speaking to her."

"Not you. You deaf sod." Sylvia swatted his arm. "She hears the land speaking to her."

"Is that so now?" Henry leaned close to Darcie and

spoke low. "You know what they say about folks who can hear the land talking to them, don't you?"

"No, what?" Darcie asked.

"I was hoping you could tell me. That's why I asked." Henry laughed at his own joke. Darcie laughed with him.

"Dad, don't tease her." Connor had asked his father to go easy on her. Did he listen to anything he said? Of course not.

"It's alright. I thought it was funny," Darcie said.

"Any Irish woman who can't take a joke isn't worth the time to know, I say. You visit any time, lass. Feel free to leave my son at home if you like. I'll take you walking in the fields, and you can tell me what they're saying. Aye?" Henry winked and gave Connor a look of approval.

Darcie had won over the O'Brian's in an instant.

CHAPTER 14

DARCIE OFFERED to help Sylvia in the kitchen. They returned with their arms full of sandwiches, fruits, cheeses, brown bread, and butter. When Connor offered to make Darcie a plate, Henry and Sylvia glanced at each other with knowing looks. He'd never been so attentive to anyone else.

Darcie took a piece of bread, slathered it with butter, and unconsciously hummed as she took a bite. She stopped chewing when she realized all the blue eyes at the table were watching her. She placed the bread on her plate.

Henry slammed his palm on the table. His booming laughter bounced around the room. "Connor, you found yourself a keeper! Any woman who can appreciate good butter like that is bang on in my book!"

Connor whispered, "Did you know you were humming?"

"Was I?" Darcie shrunk into her chair. "I never hum. How embarrassing." She looked across the table and apologized.

Connor was about to work his magic when he was

interrupted by Sylvia. She wasn't about to allow a guest in her home feel inadequate. And Connor wasn't the only one with a magic touch.

"Humming means you're happy. There's nothing embarrassing about being happy. So, no apology necessary." Sylvia gave Connor a nod. Her kind words did the trick.

They spoke about Connor's work, family gossip, and Henry and Sylvia's recent trip to Spain—the weather was fine, the wine was not.

When they had finished eating, Darcie helped clean the dishes. She washed while Sylvia dried. "Your plates are beautiful." Darcie admired the blue and white china. Each plate was hand painted with a bouquet of flowers in the center and bordered with a Celtic knot.

"Thank you. We've broken a few, but there are still enough to bring out when someone special comes to tea." Sylvia placed the plate in the drying rack. "I hope we see you again. How long are you staying?"

"I don't know." *Maybe forever.*

Sylvia put down her towel. "It's not my way to interfere with my son's life, but I see the way he is with you. You two are like magnets. He speaks to you with a deep understanding. And he's never looked at anyone the way he looks at you. Not even that doxie he dated for so long. I was glad to see the back of her! But you—there's something special about you." She laid a hand on Darcie's arm. "Promise me one thing?"

"Of course."

"Don't break my son's heart. If you're in this for a bit of fun, then you had better tell him now."

Darcie didn't know what to say. Sylvia had practically

said that Connor was in love with her. She couldn't deny that Sylvia's words tugged at her heart. "The truth is," she stammered. "I know I just met him, and I know this will sound crazy, but I—"

She was cut off by Connor peeking his head into the kitchen doorway, inviting her on a walk.

Sylvia and Henry watched through the kitchen window as their son and this charming woman walked hand in hand through the field in perfect rhythm. Connor kissed her hand and ran away, leaving Darcie to chase him down. Her braid bounced as she jumped into his waiting arms, falling him over. They had never seen their son so happy.

When it was time to leave, Darcie was sad to go. Henry and Sylvia were kind and she would have been happy to spend the day with them.

"Thank you for having me in your home and for the delicious lunch. I promise I won't hum if I come again," Darcie teased.

Henry pulled Darcie up in a bear hug. "I meant what I said. You're welcome here anytime. Especially if you hum, aye."

Sylvia reached up for a hug and spoke for only Darcie to hear. "I know what you were trying to say. Love, at first sight, is a rare gift from fate, my dear. Don't throw it away." She patted her back and spoke louder. "It was a pleasure, and Henry is right, you are always welcome here."

Darcie put on her sunglasses to hide her tears. "Thank you."

Connor held Darcie's hand as they walked to the car, where he opened the door for her. She turned and waved goodbye. "What was my mother whispering to you?"

"I asked for her brown bread recipe. She said she would mail it to me."

Connor knew Darcie was lying. But he saw the look in his mother's eyes when she hugged Darcie. Whatever it was, it was said out of love. He wouldn't press the matter. Yet.

"Where are you whisking me away to now?" she asked.

"Skellig, where they have delicious chocolate. How does that sound? Will that make you hum?"

"I'm never going to live that down, am I?"

CHAPTER 15

AFTER THE SKELLIGS CHOCOLATE SHOP, where Darcie nearly cleared them out of their supply, they went on to the Kerry Cliffs. Connor handed her the wellies he had brought along and draped her sweater over his arm in case she needed it. It was just about sunset when they reached the top of the cliffs.

"This is amazing! What a view!"

"Aye, it is grand," he agreed proudly. "I think these cliffs have more character than Moher. Out there in the distance are the Skellig Islands. Skellig means steep rock. Appropriate, don't you think? The larger of the two is Skellig Michael. It has an old monastery on it. The other is Little Skellig."

The two islands were sharp and jagged, rising up from the sea like mighty beacons. But they looked desolate. She couldn't imagine a body living on the island.

"Why did they build a monastery there?"

"I don't know. It was a hard living, to be sure. Vikings attacked the monks. They murdered many of the monks and stole their holy relics. They would have been safer here on the mainland than sitting ducks out there. But hey, what do I know?" He shrugged his shoulders. "A few tourists have died falling from those steep rocks over the years. Growing up, we would hear about another careless tourist taking the plunge to their death."

"That's grim."

"Ireland can be grim. That's life, you know. You can't have the light without the dark, love without loss, beauty without... some feckin eejit tourist who fancies themselves the next Indiana Jones."

Darcie burst out laughing. "That was a poetic speech you were making until the end."

"Things were getting dark with talk of Vikings slaughtering monks and all. Thought I would lighten the mood a bit."

Ireland, her devastating beauty tells you that it cannot fully be appreciated until you have been broken and then she will make you weep. Thousands of years of invaders all coming for the beauty, fighting for this rugged, treacherous, breathtaking bounty that can be found in no other place. It was easy for Darcie to see why the monks would choose to live on that desolate rock. Look at the view they would have had. They were kings with a front-row seat.

A small, dark cloud settled in overhead, misting them with rain and creating a brilliant double rainbow hanging high above stretching out into the valley. Darcie bounced toward it to take a picture. Connor had to admit it was a stunner. He smiled to himself. From where he was standing, she looked like she was right at the end of the rainbow.

There's my treasure. He took his phone out and snapped a picture. *That's one for the books.*

The sun had set over the distant islands, streaking the sky in vivid orange, pink, yellow, and purple. It did not disappoint. Darcie tucked herself under Connor's arm and hummed. The day could not have been more perfect. She wished it could go on forever.

Connor looked up at the sky. Not a cloud to be seen. "There is one more place to show you."

"But it's nearly dark."

"Trust me. You'll love it."

CONNOR HAD PUT the top up on the Cadillac before they left the cliffs. It was getting cooler now that the sun had gone down. He parked the car near Ballinsskelligs Beach where they could see the ruins of McCarthy's Tower in the distance and set the top back down, only to reveal a night sky that had more stars than she had seen in her whole life. Darcie could see the Milky Way, and it was positively wondrous.

"This is spectacular!" She gazed in awe at all the stars. "You were right. You can't have light without darkness. I've looked up at the night sky many times, but never have I seen something like this."

"You're not humming." He teased lightly with stars dancing in his bright eyes. "You must not like it too much." He looked around, checking if they were alone. Seeing as they were, he slid across the seat, taking her in his arms. "Let's see if I can get you to hum for me."

He took her down in a deep kiss, and she hummed sweet and low.

As he kissed her senseless, all Darcie could hear playing in her mind was: *I could take you to paradise up above ... tell me I'm the only one* ... life would be a dream, sweetheart ...

She held him tight as she melted into the leather, humming the tune into his mouth.

HE HAD EARLIER TURNED the oldies radio station back on for the drive home. She swayed to the music and daydreamed with a smile of a cat that just ate all the cream.

"What's put that smile on your face?"

"You." He smiled back appreciatively. "I haven't been parking in over twenty years. Nice touch, O'Brian."

He liked the nickname. "I always aim to please. I wanted to do a whole lot more to you than kissing, you know?"

"Yes. But you didn't. Leaving a girl breathless and wanting more, that's sexy. Just, don't make a habit of it."

Connor's mouth dropped open. Darcie reached over and casually closed it for him while singing along with the radio. He didn't know what or who a "Sloopy" was, but it made Darcie happy, and that was enough for him.

"CONNOR, TODAY WAS PERFECT. THANK YOU," Darcie said, disappointed that their day was over.

He pulled her into him, and soon she was drowning in

another deep kiss. He had her moaning as he dipped his tongue in and out threaded his hands in her hair.

"Breathless now?"

Feeling a little woozy, she blinked her eyes open. "Wow."

"My job here is done." He took her hand. "Sweet dreams, Darcie."

"Good night, Connor," she said in a dreamy voice. She hadn't gained her bearings back from their interlude.

Connor smiled, patting himself on the back. As he slowly drove away, he sang, "Life would be a dream, sweetheart."

Darcie floated up to her room and leaned against the inside of her door, releasing a rosy sigh. *That was one hell of a woo.*

CHAPTER 16

CONNOR and his crew were taking a break outside the hotel in the back. A cute young blonde passed by. The men watched her walk past with mild interest.

"Nah, she's too young and trying too hard. Look at that war paint. High maintenance, that one!" Tom said.

"Did any of you see that hot local woman in the blue Mercedes staying here?" Mack whistled. "She wasn't wearing a ring."

"I heard she's American," said Tom.

"Oh, no?" said Dermot. "I'll race you to see who gets to her first to propose marriage. She could be straight from the pit of Hell and I would gladly burn in her fire."

"Don't you have your third kid on the way?" asked Duff, slapping Dermot's back.

"A man can dream, can't he?"

"Hey, boss, you want in on this wager?" asked Trevor.

Duff put his arm over Trevor's shoulder. "Don't bother Trev, he never does. You're new, but you'll soon learn that he's no time for the ladies or the likes of our games. And more's the pity."

"That's a damn crying shame," said Tully. "A woman like that could convert me."

Connor knew Darcie was out for a walk on the hotel grounds and considering the attention she was getting he thought now would be a good time to make things between them official. He sent her a text inviting her to come and meet the guys.

Mack stood up from sitting on the bench. "Look, here she comes!"

They all lowered their voices as she approached from across the lawn, each with a daffy smile on his face.

Is that what I look like? Connor stood behind his men and waved to Darcie in the distance.

"Jesus, look at that smile of hers," said Dermot. "If any man looks at my daughter the way I just looked at her, I'll feed him to the pigs."

"She could be a giant ball of crazy," said Trev.

"No way. With those angel eyes?" Tom said.

"Her mouth must taste like nectar," said Mack, wiping his brow with his sleeve.

"She could be whatever she wants with me!" said Tom.

"I wouldn't mind getting lost in that wild mane of hers every morning," mused Duff.

"How's a woman like that not taken?" asked Tully. "If she were mine, I wouldn't let her out of the house!"

"And that's why you're single!"

They all laughed.

Before the crew could say anything more, Connor parted the way between them, walked directly to Darcie, and dipped her in a kiss leaving the men dumbfounded, with their jaws hanging open and heads tilted.

"Hi there, baby. You busy tonight?" Connor asked.

"What did you have in mind?"

"Wanna marry me?"

"Hmmm, you are very handsome, but I need a little convincing," she said with a playful smile as she pulled him down.

Connor nearly dropped her when his arms went limp. As far as she was concerned, it was no less than he deserved for teasing her.

"That's my girl. Want to meet the lads?" He stood her up. "We were just talking about you," he said loudly.

They each took off their hard hat, holding them reverently while Darcie was introduced. She shook each man's hand, repeating their names so she wouldn't forget them, and gave them all a genuine, warm smile. Even as each one bit their tongue from saying the first thing, they all thought: *She's an American!*

Each revered that she was even more lovely than any of them imagined.

As she walked away, each of them turned to Connor and handed him their money. Duff was last in the line. He grabbed a hold of Connor and kissed him square on the mouth. "It's about time, Boss! You lucky bastard."

CHAPTER 17

Darcie was sound asleep when the phone rang the morning of her birthday. She poked her arm out from under the duvet, blindly feeling around for the phone. Finding it, she dragged it under the blanket and answered in a muffled, groggy croak.

"I woke you? Sorry," Connor said.

"It's alright. You did me a favor." She looked at the time with one eye open. "I have an appointment at the spa in an hour. I must have forgotten to set my alarm."

"Will you remember how to find the place, or would you like me to come and take you?"

"I'm not so drowsy that I didn't pick up on that innuendo, O'Brian, and yes, I know how to find it. I think."

"Do you have plans for this evening? I was going to ask you to dinner."

"That would be nice."

"I'll pick you up at five."

"Alright. See you," she said with another long yawn.

She hung up and tossed the phone out from under the

blankets, pulling the covers back over her head for a few more minutes of shut-eye. Turning forty was exhausting.

DARCIE DECIDED TO INDULGE HERSELF. That was something she hadn't done in ages. She hardly left any spa treatment untouched. Although she drew the line at cryotherapy. Why anyone would pay to be frozen was beyond her. Instead, she poached in the private, outdoor hot tub overlooking the lake until she turned into a prune.

As she enjoyed the view, she began to think how nice it would have been to have Sondra with her. It had been so long since she had a girlfriend, it hadn't crossed her mind to invite her along. Next time.

By the time she was supposed to get dressed for dinner, she was so relaxed she could hardly stand. She slipped on a dress, put on a light smudge of lipstick and a wisp of mascara. They had done her hair along with the hot oil treatment. It didn't look quite as lovely as when they did it, thanks to her extra-long soak and shower, but she decided it still looked good.

"You're looking well and pampered. How was the spa?" he asked, holding her car door open.

"Wonderful," she purred as she poured like liquid into the car. "It was exactly what I wanted to do on my birthday."

"Today is your birthday? You didn't tell me."

"I'm sorry, I didn't think it was a big deal."

He had to keep up his charade only a little longer. "Well, sure, it was a big enough deal for you to travel around the world on your own to celebrate. But not important enough for you to tell me." He got in the car and laid his hands on the steering wheel. "You didn't think I would enjoy celebrating with you?"

"I hadn't thought about it like that." She laid a hand over his shoulder. "My birthday hasn't been a day to celebrate in a long time. I'm not used to someone making any fuss over me."

"What life did you have in America where no one cared about your birthday?"

"It wasn't that no one cared. I just had a quiet life." She shrugged her shoulders. "I'm sorry I upset you. It was an honest mistake." She said in a sugar-laced apologetic voice.

He flashed a devilish grin. "You can find a way to make it up to me later."

"That's a dirty trick to get me into bed."

"Darcie, I can't believe you would accuse me of taking advantage of a situation like that!"

"I'm sorry. I thought you were teasing me."

He smirked.

"Oh, you!"

CHAPTER 18

"WELCOME TO MY HUMBLE HOME," said Connor.

"This is your house?" He took her hand, walking her to the front door.

"Make yourself at home. I have kitchen work to do."

It was as if he had dipped into her dreams and plucked out her ideal house. The foyer had a vaulted ceiling with a large but not overbearing black iron chandelier. The rooms were large, open with high ceilings and wood floors. The colors reminded her of sand, wood, water, and sky. The living room had a stone fireplace in the center that reached to the ceiling. Connor explained that it was a gas fireplace whose switch was connected to a generator. Sometimes the thunderstorms were wicked there near the sea. The back wall was glass that looked out onto a large yard where she could make out a horizon in the distance. The serenity enveloped her.

Connor knew where she was in the house when he heard her screech. He smiled to himself.

As she walked through the house admiring and poking

around, she found herself inside his bathroom. On the edge of the sink was a new purple toothbrush placed beside a new dental floss container. Inside the shower was her shampoo, soap, and a sea sponge. All new, but placed as if they had been there all along.

Beside his bed was a dainty bouquet of garden flowers in a crystal vase on the right side of the bed, her side these days. He had taken great care in making her feel at home. She wondered where he got the flowers. They smelled wonderful and drifted her off into a daydream where she was home and safe and happy here with him.

It felt real. It was so clear in her mind's eye, clear as the exquisite Waterford crystal vase in her hands. She let it fill her up and didn't push it away. Today was her birthday, and she was determined to savor every moment of it without question.

She opened the small drawer of the bedside table. Inside was each cream that Sondra insisted every woman needed. Darcie had thought them unnecessary, but, after using them, had to admit she loved the indulgence. Connor was feeding that indulgence.

He hadn't missed anything. *I wouldn't be surprised if I opened the closet and found a replica of my clothes.* She threw open the door with a secret giggle and scrunched her face when all she found beside his clothes was a silk bathrobe and matching slippers for her. *No nightgown, O'Brian?*

She began making her way back into the kitchen, from where a heavenly scent was wafting through the air, when a painting on the wall struck her eye. A storm was just beginning to break with a ripple of sunlight over the local cliffs painted in brilliant shades of blue. In the corner was the title "This Too Shall Pass."

Her heart was in her throat. She wanted to climb into the safety of his arms and tell him she loved him. She had stumbled on love on her journey seeking peace. But she was never going to have peace, was she? Not until she told Connor the truth.

Back in the kitchen she watched him slicing fruit, such a domestic, simple act, but it was for her. No need to spoil dinner. *I will talk to him after.*

She took the knife from his hand, placing it on the counter. "Thank you," she said and kissed him long and tender.

"You must really like that toothbrush."

"Actually, it was the floss that impressed me. I don't need anything back at the hotel. Keep spoiling me, and I'll never leave."

He slanted his eyes up from slicing. *That's the point, darling.* "I wanted everything to be special for you. Did I go overboard?"

"Maybe. But I love … it all."

She loves me. I know it. Well, if she doesn't want to admit it yet, that's fine. I have more tricks up my sleeve. He picked the knife up and continued slicing with a coy smile. "Did you like your flowers?"

"They're beautiful. Where did you get them?"

"My garden. You will see later. I had some help from your Sondra with the robe and such."

"Your home is wonderful."

"Thank you. I designed it myself."

"Seems large for a bachelor."

"I don't plan on being alone forever." He drilled her with his eyes.

She blushed and looked out the window.

"What were you making the fuss about?" he asked as he uncorked a bottle of wine.

"That is the nicest shower I've ever seen! How many heads are there? I wanted to turn on every single one to see what they do."

He chuckled. "I knew you would like my home and especially my shower after you said how much you enjoyed your spa day. We had a job building a spa that wanted that shower. I was building this place at the time and thought, why not make myself one? It's grand when I've a knot in my shoulder. You can give it a go tomorrow."

"You're presuming I'll stay with you tonight?"

He opened the oven, pulled out a perfect roast chicken with vegetables, and placed it in front of her. "I would like it very much if you stayed."

"How can I say no when you ask so nicely?"

CHAPTER 19

"That was a delicious dinner, thank you." Darcie got up from the table to look out the window. The sun was going to set soon. "Not to insult Flynn, but I enjoyed your cooking more."

"About that." Connor motioned for her to follow him. "I have a confession. I had some help with dinner." He opened the trash bin to reveal a mass of what at one time had been some sort of food but was now so charred it would need a carbon date to prove anything. "Grace is the one whose food you love. I knew not to ask Flynn. We don't need anything else jellied, dehydrated, or served with seaweed."

"Connor, this is all ..." She dabbed her eyes, trying not to cry. "It's all so perfect, and you went to all this trouble."

"I would do anything to make you smile. And I am failing if you keep crying, acushla." He wiped her tears.

"You asked Grace and Sondra to help you, and they did. All of you went to so much trouble. I can't say how grateful

I am. I loved them the moment we met, you know? They felt like people I'd known my whole life."

"I know the feeling," he said.

She smiled back, nodding her head. It was all so easy with him. But she needed to tell him the truth. She drank the last of her wine and had started to speak when he presented her with two slices of chocolate cake.

"I ruined your cake the other night asking you about your family while you ate, so I thought I could make it up to you. It's from a local bakery."

"I thought you didn't like chocolate."

"What makes you say that?"

"The joke you made about the girl guide. I thought that meant you don't like chocolate."

"I love chocolate. But I hate those biscuits."

"I don't remember you having any at the chocolate shop."

"You're joking! You were clearing that place out. I was afraid of getting my hand bitten off if I touched a piece!"

She laughed, taking a bite of her cake. "This is the best cake ever. You should hide yours before I steal it."

"If you think I'll allow you to steal mine, you've another thought coming. Birthday or no." His eyes dared her.

She perched herself on his lap, draping her arms around his neck, and mustered up the most pathetic look she could. "You don't mean that, do you?"

"I most certainly do."

She nibbled his bottom lip. "Really?"

"Really. Nothing comes between an O'Brian and his cake." He was fighting a losing battle.

She kissed him deeper while she reached behind her for a scoop of his cake and slung her hand full onto his face.

He had felt her move her arm and suspected what she was up to. "That how it is then?" he asked as he wiped a glob from his cheek and licked his fingers.

"Yes, love."

"Come here, you." He locked her in his arms, laughing as she tried to escape. "I thought you wanted my cake?" He caught her with his chocolate-smudged face and kissed her face all over, not missing one single inch.

She ran a finger up her cheek and licked it. "This really is the best chocolate cake I've ever had."

CHAPTER 20

CONNOR'S HOUSE was near the sea. He had an expansive backyard that seemed to go on forever. Darcie could hear the waves in the breeze and could smell the saltwater.

She breathed in deep. "That is my favorite sound."

"The sea speaking to you, love?" he asked as he brought her close to his side, resting her head on his shoulder.

"Just the sound of the waves and the salty breeze. It's all so soothing." He led her to the top of a short cliff that over-looked the beach. "It's so perfect."

"Aye, it is at that." He was looking at her, not the beach. "The path down to the beach isn't a hard walk, but I won't take you down there tonight. The sun is setting, and it will be too dark to see the way. I'll take you there tomorrow if you like."

"Yes, I would."

He took her hand to walk back to the house. "There's one last place to show you." He led her through an area of trees that opened into a large garden with a beautifully made rotunda in the center.

"You have a secret garden?"

"Yes, I suppose you could call it that."

"It's like stepping into a fairyland."

He watched her as she gazed around with delight, taking in all the colors and scents of the flowers that all joined in a chorus of pure beauty. "Come, sit with me."

They sat on a bench under the rotunda lit by delicate lights, making their surroundings appear even more enchanted. Darcie thought she might cry from all the beauty. She started to speak when Connor pulled a gift from under their seat.

"Happy birthday."

"You said you didn't know today was my birthday."

He shrugged his shoulders.

She smiled, and while she thought about saying he didn't need to give her anything, she decided against it. She hadn't been given a present in years, and she loved presents.

He handed her a slim, velvet, emerald green box wrapped with a gold bow. She carefully opened it to find a gold necklace with an intricate Celtic knot pendant. The very one she had fallen for at the jewelry store window. She looked closely. There was a charm on the clasp that read "You are mine, I am yours" in Gaelic.

"Connor, this is so beautiful! How did you know?"

"Know what?"

"I saw this when I was out shopping. Something about it spoke to me. I nearly bought it."

"It caught my eye through the window when I went to buy your wellies. I thought it would look perfect around your neck."

She turned so he could put the necklace on her. She turned back to him, tears now flowing down her face.

"Aye, so it does." He kissed her eyelids and cheeks. "Looks like fate played a part in your present. No need to cry."

What were the odds of him buying this one necklace? She had to admit that the idea of fate was beginning to make a home in her heart. She held the pendant in her hand, admiring the beauty of it. Her eyes focused on the two hearts in the center. It was speaking to her of true love. True love that she betrayed with each passing minute with her lies. It was time.

"There's something I have to tell you."

He swept his hand across her face and cradled her head. "Shhh, not tonight. It can wait for tomorrow," he urged. "Tonight is for us."

Her worries became watercolors running down a page, as she forgot all else and surrendered.

WITHOUT A WORD, he walked her back to the house, where he carried her across the threshold. He placed her down and looked on her lovingly. He was going to take his time. Taste her, savor her and drive them both crazy before he had her.

No rushing. Not this time.

He lit candles that were placed around the bedroom. Their real purpose was for use during a storm and the electricity went out, but they would suit this night perfectly.

She reached for him as he undressed and watched him in the flickering light. He was magnificent.

"What's that I see in your eyes?" he asked.

"I was just thinking how beautiful you are."

"Beautiful, am I?"

She nodded and began undressing, trying her best not to feel self-conscious.

"I want to do that." He unzipped her dress, letting it slip to the floor, and placed a lingering kiss on her shoulder as he put his arm around her waist, easing close.

Jesus, how had he lived without her until now? She fit so perfectly against him, inside his arms.

He laid over her, showering her with sweet kisses and Irish murmurs of love. He worked his way down and he gently slid off her underwear.

She lay there naked in his bed. The candlelight dancing on her skin, reflecting off her hair and in her eyes.

"Darcie, you're the most beautiful woman I've ever seen, and that's the truth."

Her creamy skin turned pink all over. He had not seen that before. He had not taken the time to notice. That was all going to change.

Being with her was like coming home. He caressed her soft skin and placed a kiss on the childhood scar she bore on her leg. "How did you get this?"

"The car accident that killed my parents."

"My Darcie. You've been through so much." He lightly scraped his whiskered cheek against the soft skin between her thighs.

Her eyes flew open. "Connor ... "

He looked at her anxious expression. "You want me to stop?" he asked after kissing her silky skin.

Her lips parted, but no reply came out.

"Do you trust me?"

"Yes."

"Acushla, let me pleasure you." He slid a hand up her stomach. "Take my hand." Holding his hand always set her at ease.

He was thoroughly pleased with himself when her eyes rolled back in her head as she sobbed his name.

No other man had given her so much, made her feel so much, or made her want to give so much back, and she trusted him absolutely.

He laid his hands on her shoulders and ran them down her arms, linking their hands. "Look at me. I want to see your eyes when you come with me," he said.

Their slow rhythm was like music. Everything in the world disappeared as they rose and fell together.

All she could hear was him. All she could feel was love, and her body began to hum when he whispered, "You are mine, I am yours," as they slid over the edge together.

LATER, Connor murmured with pleasure in his sleep. Darcie had woken up and kissed her way down his navel and took him in her mouth.

His eyes flew open. "Darcie! You—" He stopped talking and let the sensation flow through him. He looked at her, and his desire heightened. He gently tugged her shoulders.

"As nice as this is, I would prefer you on my lap and in my arms. Now," he said, pulling her up against his body.

She shied away.

"What is it?" he asked.

"Was I doing it wrong?"

Connor, dumbfounded at the weighted question, wasn't sure what to address first. The fact that she asked or the underlying fact that she had never done that before and what that might also mean.

She tried to pull away when he caught her arms. Embarrassed, she wouldn't look at him. He rested his hand against her cheek.

"You were doing it right, more than right. I just want to hold you in my arms for right now. Would that be okay?"

She nodded her head, wishing she could hide. The night had been perfect until that moment when she ruined it.

Connor thought about how to address the matter. He needed to choose his words carefully. "Darcie, I have something I want to ask you."

"Okay."

"You told me you had not been with anyone in a long time. What did that mean, exactly?" He could feel her tension. He started to comb his fingers through her hair to calm her, but she wouldn't answer. "I think what it meant was you've been very selective of who you took to your bed and that someone along the way let you down."

"Yes," she replied in a small voice.

He said nothing, waiting for a better answer. She tried to pull away, but he anticipated that and held her steady. "You trust me, don't you?"

"Of course."

"Then you know you can tell me anything. Talk to me, acushla." He resumed combing her hair and waited.

"I had boyfriends in college and later on. I liked being near them, but I didn't see what all the fuss was about. I didn't really get any pleasure from any of it, so I put myself on the shelf."

"So, you had never found pleasure with a man?"

She stayed quiet a moment. "No." She closed her eyes.

"Darcie, I knew there was something special about you, about us, when I met you. You had a hold over me the moment I saw you. When I took you inside the ruins, I wanted you more than I had wanted anything in my life. I meant what I said, I shouldn't have taken advantage of you that night."

She opened her mouth to interrupt.

"But I did. And I'm not sorry for it."

Darcie looked at him, confused. Connor lifted her chin.

"You heard me right. I'm not sorry for it. Maybe you didn't tell me no, but I could have walked away."

"I didn't want you to walk away."

"I could see that in your eyes. I couldn't resist you. And now that I know you had never known what it's like to lose yourself, well, I'm not sorry that lucky man was me. I know I teased you the next day when you fell out of the elevator."

"I didn't fall out of the elevator. I dropped my bags and tripped." She had to preserve some dignity.

He smiled. "Yes, well, do you remember what I said?"

"You said I wasn't a woman who goes sneaking around with men."

"But you did with me."

She nodded her head.

"Why?"

"Because ... I felt something special between us. Something I'd never felt before. I didn't understand it, still don't understand it. I only know that... I need you."

"Aye. I need you too."

"You do?"

"Yes. I do." He kissed her, sealing his word.

"Would you like a drink? I'm going to get some water."

He started to get up when she caught his waist, urging him to stay. "I read a poem once that described two lovers as being consumed by fire. I didn't know what it meant. I do now. I was consumed that night and have been ever since."

It was as close as she could bring herself to saying the three words she wanted to say and he so desperately wanted to hear.

Connor's heart nearly burst. Slowly, she wound her arms around him, feeling every muscle under her fingertips as she laid back, pulling him with her. That water would have to wait.

DARCIE CRAWLED INTO BED, handing over a glass of water. She snuggled herself in the curve of his arm, his favorite place for her to be.

"Why have you turned so many women down?"

Connor spurted out his water. He was trying to have a moment with her, and she was teasing him. He liked this side of her, so he took the bait. "What makes you think I do?"

"Sondra," she said.

"Girl talk, is it?"

"She told me you're one of the most successful businessmen in the county." She looked up at him through her eyelashes. "You are modest, not telling me that yourself. She tried to get you to notice her once, but you didn't."

It was Connor's turn to blush. He wasn't used to people talking about his success.

"She also said that you're 'bleeding massive' and that I need to be myself around you, and then she sold me more underwear."

"You told her I tore your underwear?" He wasn't sure whether to be embarrassed or not.

"Yes. She figured out the rest for herself and asked me if you were good or not," she said, giggling. "I haven't had a girlfriend to talk to in so long. I felt like a gossiping teenager."

He hugged her closer. "I'm happy you're making friends. I know life has been lonely. That's why we should make up for lost time and give you something better to say during your next girl talk. Tickle fight!"

She squealed with laughter as he brought the sheets over their heads.

Late in the night, Connor woke with a start to Darcie screaming in her sleep for help. She was crying, and her body trembled. He moved in close and held her tight while he whispered comforting words in Irish. He wasn't sure why that worked or what made him think to do that in the first place, but it always did the trick.

Within a minute, she settled down and stopped crying. Her bad dreams were much more profound than he had thought. Whatever it was that haunted this woman, he wanted nothing more than to chase it away and keep her safe.

CHAPTER 21

WHEN MORNING CAME, Connor and Darcie laughed when they realized it wasn't morning at all. It was nearly one o'clock when they woke up. Connor got up to make tea, telling Darcie to stay in bed.

When he returned, she lay languishing in bed. He loved the look of her in his home, in his bed, and under his sheets. He laid a tray of tea, biscuits, toast, jam, butter, and fruit beside her.

"Yum. You've outdone yourself. Dinner and breakfast."

"Oh sure, and I suppose it was someone else pleasuring you all night, fulfilling your desires?"

She blushed and leaned in for a kiss with her mouth full of toast, leaving toast crumbs on his lips. "Was that you? I thought I was dreaming," she teased.

"Darcie, last night was," he wiped the crumbs from his lips and licked his finger, "it was amazing."

"That was the best birthday I've ever had. And you were amazing," she said in a rough, at best, Irish accent.

Connor roared with laughter and leaned in to kiss her ear. She squirmed as his mouth tickled her.

"Thanks for the compliment, but you don't need to use that accent."

"No good, huh?"

"You sounded like a leprechaun with emphysema."

"That's flattering. Okay, no more Irish talk for me."

Connor winked at her as he stood up. "I'm going to shower. Care to join me?"

She zoomed out of bed and past him, leaving her own shadow to catch up while she turned on all the different shower heads, giggling with delight as they pulsed, sprayed, massaged, misted, poured, and rained down.

He loved the sound of her laugh and how she expressed joy so freely. He closed his eyes a moment, taking in her sound. The night before, he had drawn every sweet, soft sigh from her body. It was music to his ears.

Her giggles turned to groans, and his mind switched gears. Picturing Darcie standing naked with her head tipped back, her long auburn hair slick against her breast, and body glistening underneath the waterfall in his shower was shoving all tender feelings to the side. He wanted to ravage her until his name echoed through tiles. He decided to test the waters.

"Aye, you'll be knowing that I'll not be so gentle as last night?" he called out.

"I'm counting on it!"

His jaw dropped. *She is full of little surprises!*

CHAPTER 22

"I PROMISED you a walk to the beach."

"I don't have anything to wear for walking down that path."

"I thought of that." He pulled out a pair of his jogging pants, a University College T-shirt, socks, and her purple wellies.

As they set out on the bright day, Darcie got a clearer look at Connor's property. "This is very large."

"You're right. It is larger than most here. Some of it is a wooded area you can see over there." He pointed off to the left. "And over to the right, there is where the entrance to the secret garden is."

"Your garden was so beautiful. Could I walk in there again?"

"Of course. Do you want to go there now?"

"No, I want to go to the water," she said happily.

"The sea calls, and we must go."

Connor led her carefully down the cliff trail, holding

onto her hand the whole way down. When they reached the bottom, she hopped down. "That trail isn't so bad."

"It can get slippery sometimes, so be careful when you come here on your own."

"I can come here by myself?"

He leaned in close, pulling her to him. "I would like it very much if you spent as much time here as you please. You look good here." He kissed her forehead. "Now go find some treasure."

She smiled and turned to walk up the beach. He had found his treasure in Darcie. How long before he could make her see that? He couldn't push her too hard. But he also couldn't live without her.

He heard her screech as a wave splashed up. *There she is, the free spirit I first fell for. I love this side of her. What is it that haunts this free spirit?* He started to hatch a plan to find out.

"I didn't find any treasure, but I found some sea glass." She held out her palm. "I know it's dumb, isn't it?"

"No. I was thinking about what I have inside that you could put that into so you can admire your collection."

"I wouldn't call this a collection."

"True. But if you keep coming back, you will find more sea glass, and eventually, it will grow into a collection."

"That would be nice."

"Ready to go back to the garden?"

"I nearly forgot about the garden."

She turned her face back to the sea and took one last deep breath. She hadn't realized how much she missed living near the water. She had grown up near the ocean but had moved away a decade before and never looked back. It had been too long.

They made their way back up the cliff path. She insisted Connor didn't need to hold her hand the whole way, but he stayed close. When they were near the top, Darcie slipped. Connor quickly grabbed hold of her before she fell.

"That came out of nowhere. I was watching every step I took. I should have held your hand. Thank you for catching me."

Connor's face had gone white with dread when he saw her slip. He pulled her tight into his arms. "I couldn't bear it if something were to happen to you." He pressed his forehead to hers. "You promise me if you come down here alone, you will be extra careful."

"I promise."

"You gave me a proper scare."

"I'm sorry. I didn't mean to be clumsy and scare you."

He relaxed. "You're not clumsy. Right then, off to the secret garden?"

THEY PASSED through moss-covered trees that were naturally shaped into a cave; she couldn't help but smile. It really was like a secret place. When the trees opened up to the garden itself, she lost her breath. It was more beautiful in the daytime than at night.

Hydrangeas were in full bloom everywhere in white, pink, and blue, roses in every color, lavender, bluebells, fairy thimbles, poppies, and so many more flowers she couldn't name. A burst of color surrounded her, and in the center was the white rotunda. She walked up its stairs and admired the craftsmanship.

"You built this?"

"I did."

"And did you plan this garden, too?"

"Yes."

"Connor, this is like heaven."

She looked out over the garden and found her thoughts drifting toward how perfect a place it would be for a wedding. She let the fantasy seep in a little before she reluctantly dragged herself back to reality. She wanted to stay. Not just here in the garden but with Connor. He kept hinting to her to stay. Maybe she could. The thought made her smile.

"What's put that smile on your face?"

"You."

"Anything about me in particular?"

She sighed. "I was thinking how nice it is to be with you. I like spending time with you."

"I like spending time with you as well. Could I spend more time with you today?"

She took his hand. "As much as you like."

They continued to walk through the garden's paths, enjoying all the blooming beauty. "Then we will have time for that talk I promised you," he said, draping his arm over her.

She halted her steps and exhaled. It was time.

"You have something to tell me. I have something I need to tell you as well."

"Let me go first. If I put this off again, I may never tell you, and I have to," she said. Stammering and fidgeting, she willed herself the strength to speak. "Truth is, I'm not here for my birthday. I'm—"

"I know."

"You know?" *How?*

"There's something you need to know. The night before you arrived here," he took her hands, "I dreamed of you. You were scared, crying, running away. I felt your fear prickling up my skin when I woke up."

She stared at his face, trying to comprehend his words.

"Truth is, I've been dreaming of you for years. I never knew who you were or where to find you. You never spoke to me. But I know you've been sad for a long time."

She had a dumbfounded expression.

"How else would I know that you never used to wear your hair down? Every time I saw you, your hair was tied back."

She touched the tips of her hair that she wore loose and long. She hadn't done that before now.

"And I know you're not here for your birthday. I didn't tell you until now because I didn't want to frighten you away. I've looked for you in every woman I see. I'd given up ever finding you, and then you appeared in the hallway. I was hoping you would know me, but you didn't."

She shook her head. This was too fantastic.

"But you sensed something. I know you did, or else you would have turned me down when I asked you out. You don't shrink away from me. You weren't afraid of me like other men. Don't you wonder why? It's because we belong together. I don't know what made you run, but I can't help but be grateful you ran to me."

Darcie stood, silent, staring at the white roses. "Fate?"

"How else can you explain us?"

"I can't. I don't know how to process this. It's a lot to take in, you know?"

"Want me to leave you alone?"

She considered less than a moment. "No. No, I don't want to be without you. I don't want space."

"I don't want space either," he said, surrounding her in his arms. "You are mine to protect, to cherish." He cupped her head into his neck and felt her shoulders drop. "You tell me why you left in your own time. I'm not going anywhere. You brave lass."

"You're right," she mumbled into his neck. "I did run away. And I don't ever want to go back."

The thought of it was too upsetting. She gripped him tight. She had intended to tell him everything then, but his revelation was making her head spin. It would have to wait. He understood and was patient.

Neither wanted to be without the other. He used that as an excellent excuse to stay that night and every other night after with her. He'd be damned if she would spend another night alone with her fear.

CHAPTER 23

"THESE FLOWERS ARE BEAUTIFUL, Darcie. You didn't have to go to the trouble." Grace said as she admired each shade of pink, yellow, and white.

"Trouble? Are you kidding? Thanks to you, Connor and I had a delicious dinner. He showed me what he burned. I don't know what it was, but I was grateful to not have to eat it." Darcie said in a low voice so as not to offend Connor's valiant effort.

"The poor man. He was fit to be tied when he called me, you know? He so wanted your birthday to be special. And was it?"

Darcie's cheeks flushed, telling Grace all she needed to know. She patted Darcie's face and winked before going into the kitchen to find a vase. Darcie sat at a table beside the window and read the day's menu.

"Nice place you chose to visit."

The menu dropped from Darcie's hands. Her mouth trembled, her air seized. An American man sat down in the empty chair opposite her.

"Much better than the prison cell I had to look at." He picked up her menu, casually reading it. "Courtesy of your father, of course." The man's nose was still crooked from when Darcie's father had broken it in a fit of rage, defending her honor.

Darcie was frozen with fear. She couldn't speak. She wanted to scream, but nothing came out.

"I wrote to you, you know? But all my letters were returned to me. It was your meddling mother, I'm sure, who did that, not you. Little Darcie wouldn't do that to me. I look forward to seeing her name in the obituaries. Sorry to hear about your father, by the way. He was a good man. Too bad he misunderstood you and me."

How did you find me? Why are you out of prison? Grace, please help me! All these questions ran through her mind, but none of them came out of her mouth.

"It was fate that I arrived at your place when you were leaving in the cab. I'd been hanging around." He picked up a piece of bread from the basket on the table and took a bite. "I've been watching you whenever I could stay out of sight, waiting to get you alone so we can have a reunion. I know this guy, Connor? That his name? I know he's just a stand-in for me. You never took another man after me. You've been waiting for me. You must have been so lonely while I was away. I won't leave you again, I promise." He caressed her hand. "I can still feel you, you know? You were so shy that you didn't make a sound, but I knew you felt what I did when I saw your tears. And now we are free to be together."

Darcie vomited on the table and fainted onto the floor.

CHAPTER 24

DARCIE'S WORLD had turned empty, black and cold. It could have been hours, it could have been days. She didn't know or care. The darkness was peaceful. There was no one who could harm her in this dark place. In the distance, she heard her name being called, but she didn't want to listen. She turned her face away and stared off into the vast nothing, waiting for death.

The doctor found no reason for her passing out and had no explanation for her remaining unconscious. Connor had a feeling she didn't want to wake up. He swore he felt her slipping away. He sat beside her bed all night, praying and worrying. He had searched for her, longed for her too long to leave her alone. And he'd be damned if he lost her to the darkness now.

He leaned close to her ear and spoke low. He called to her, begging her to wake up, and began to tell her their story and remind her of the things she loved.

She heard his voice, soft and musical, hypnotic.

"Picture our room. We're in our bed and the windows

are open. It's a bright, sunny day. Can you taste the breeze from our beach, your favorite place? The sea glass you found each time you went there, it's sitting in the vase on your bed stand."

The darkness around her was lifted. She took in the briny air that was laced with flowers from the garden. She heard birdsong and bees and distant waves lapping against the beach, their beach. She could almost see the flowers dancing on the sea, like little fairies on the water. It was wonderful. She smelled the sheets. It was the familiar clean scent. She ran her hands around her and felt the soft blanket she liked so much and she saw a faded image of Connor, lying in bed beside her. His eyes beckoned to her.

"Our house; I built it for you. How I knew what you would want I cannot explain, it was a feeling I had. It's been waiting for you. No one was going to live there but you. It's your home. See your favorite chair by the fireplace where you like to read? That was placed there only for you.

Think to the first time we met ... I was lost to you. And our trip down The Ring. What a perfect day that was, aye? You chased me through the cold water ... I asked you to stay. Your birthday was beautiful. There in our bed, you gave me all of your body."

Listening to his thick honey voice, she was captivated. She laid still and allowed his words to fill her mind. As he went on, and all that was left was light, she saw it. She wasn't alone and scared. He was standing beside her. She felt hope rise with his assurance that he was never going to leave. She blinked her eyes.

"There she is." He could have done a weep of joy. He laid his hand across her forehead. "You're in the hospital."

She coughed. "How long have I been here?"

Connor poured her a cup of water. "Since yesterday."

She reached for his hand after taking a sip. "You look so tired."

"I'm fine, but I wouldn't say no if you offered to share your bed with me. I've been in this chair all night."

She made room.

"That's better." He said when she laid her head on his chest. In truth, he had only wanted to be near her. Sitting beside her bed waiting for her to wake up was the worst feeling he'd experienced in his life.

Connor took Darcie home with him. She refused to speak about the incident at Grace's. He didn't want to push her too hard, but knew something was very wrong. During the night, she had nightmares worse than ever before. This couldn't go on. Something needed to be done.

CHAPTER 25

DARCIE'S PHONE RANG, and she nearly leaped out of her skin. Connor had reluctantly agreed to go to work for a short while on the condition that she not leave the house. She was happy to sleep a day away. Grouchy, she answered the phone.

"Well, that's a fine hello."

"Connor!" She got chipper.

"That's better. What are you doing? Other than scaring people off your phone."

"I was sleeping, as promised."

"Would you like to come out with me?"

"I thought you had to work."

"Things here are well in hand. I can take the afternoon. There's a place I would like to show you."

After a debate about whether or not she was fit to drive herself, Connor relented. They made a plan to meet at his office. She would drive his car. He grumbled about that under his breath and prayed she didn't crash. She hadn't driven much in Ireland and, from what he had seen of her driving, he couldn't fathom how she ever got her license in the first place.

Darcie arrived at Connor's office. She hadn't been inside before and was looking forward to seeing the place. She spotted Connor with his back to her beside the tea and coffee.

She crept up behind him, stood on her tiptoes, and whispered something so uncharacteristically lewd even she was shocked. He turned around with a coy smile, and she froze. The face looking back at her was clean-shaven, with bright blue eyes and vague signs of a once broken nose.

"No need to be shy and run now, sweetheart. If that's what you want to do with me, I'm all yours. Unless, of course, you would like me to do that to you instead? I'm game for anything you have in mind."

She was scared to death. The stranger would have seen that if he had stopped to look at her face instead of every-thing else.

"I prefer blondes, but I won't mind taking a bite out of you, gingersnap," he said, reaching for her waist.

Finally, she slowly backed away, shaking.

"Jesus Christ! You're Darcie, aren't you?" he said in a panicked revelation when he saw tears fill her eyes. He held his hands out low in front of him in submission. "Love, I'm sorry. I would never have … "

Her lip began to tremble when she bumped into a desk.

"Shite." He looked around for Connor, but there was no sight of him. "Darcie, I'm Simon, Connor's cousin. He told me all about you, love. I'm not going to hurt you. I'm going to back away now, alright?"

She watched him warily as he took a few steps away,

backward, and tripped right over a trash can landing him flat on his back surrounded by wads of paper and used tea bags.

"Sure, and this is grand," he laid his head back with a thump, staring at the ceiling. "First, I make a pass at my cousin's woman and frighten the life out of her. And now," he plucked a sticky note from his forehead, "I lay here on my office floor with the trash. Could the day get any better?" He read the message and rolled his eyes: "Call mum." "Where the hell is Connor?" Simon stayed on the floor, wondering what else he could do when he heard a snort. He lifted his head, and sure enough, Darcie was trying desperately to stifle a chuckle.

"And what are you laughing at?" He raised his eyebrows. At least she wasn't screaming. "It's fine. Laugh all you like, love. I'll lay here for your amusement." He fingered out a wet tea bag from his hair, tossing it aside, making her laugh harder.

Seeing she was not in any danger, she offered her hand to help him up.

"Are we friends, then?" he asked, accepting her hand.

"I'm sorry, Simon."

"No need to apologize. The fault was mine."

"You looked like Connor," she said as she picked up the tipped trash bin and helped clean up.

"We get that a lot. When we were lads, we looked so alike that we would take each other's exams in school." Simon said, as he took the trash bin from her and placed it back on the floor. "I would do his science, and him, my history. We even swapped dates sometimes. The girls had no idea."

Simon sat her at his desk and made them each a cup of tea. By the time Connor walked in from the back with Nan, Darcie and Simon were huddled over his desk, giggling while he told stories of their childhood. Connor was pleased with the sight. At least she was laughing, which was a marked improvement from the night before. This would make their afternoon easier.

"Here's the man himself," announced Simon, as Connor leaned down to kiss Darcie.

"I see you two have been introduced. And what were you laughing about?"

Simon and Darcie glanced at each other with a grin and together chimed, "Nothing."

"Out of my way, you feckless baboon!" Nan said, shoving between Connor and Darcie.

"Alright, you old nag!" Connor stepped back. "Darcie, this is Nan. The giant pain in my—"

Darcie interrupted, giving Connor a scold for his attitude. "It's nice to meet you, Nan."

"She's too good for you," Nan said to Connor. "Noses out, you two. We've woman business to discuss." She dragged Darcie away with their arms linked. "You poor dear, I hope that ape is taking good care of you. Now, I'll make you a proper cup of tea, and you tell Nan all about yourself. Connors kept you a great secret, you know?"

Darcie looked over her shoulder. Connor and Simon waved goodbye, twinkling their fingers.

CHAPTER 26

CONNOR DROVE Darcie into the mountains and parked beside a vast field. Darcie had drifted off to sleep on the drive. "We're here," he nudged.

She looked around. It was a warm, sunny day with a kiss of a breeze through the mountains. The rolling, full, green fields were dotted with sheep and short stone walls that made up paddocks. Such a simple landscape, but still, it was majestic.

When they got to a field gate, Connor helped her climb over and plopped her and her purple wellies square into a mud puddle. She turned around to see him open the gate for himself and walkthrough. He looked at her and started laughing. She tried to tackle him.

"That perked you up."

"Is that why you made me climb that gate? To get me perky? That's a dirty trick to play on someone my age."

"Your age! You make it sound like you're ninety-seven."

She walked forward, hunched over.

"I don't know what you're playing at, but the woman

who was languishing in my bed the other day was certainly not old. Come on, grannie, we've not much further."

He put his arm around her waist, bringing her in for a hug. The fresh air and a walk were exactly what they needed. And if his plan went accordingly, it would be just the atmosphere to coax her into talking.

Ahead, she saw a footpath through the hills. "Where does this lead to?"

"Would you be talking about us or the footpath, love?" He winked.

She laughed easily. "I was referring to the footpath."

"That is a surprise. I think you'll like it."

She grabbed hold of his hand. "I've been happy so far with your surprises," she said, giving him a quick peck before skipping ahead.

She was relaxed. He couldn't avoid the subject anymore. After what Simon had told him of his encounter with Darcie and her fainting, he knew it was time. "Simon said you mistook him for me."

She stopped and looked at the ground.

"He feels terrible."

"I know. I'm not upset with Simon. It wasn't his fault."

"Darcie, I think it's time we talk about why you came here."

"Is that why we're here in the middle of a field? You think I'll pour my heart out, and nobody will hear but you?"

"There is something here I want you to see. We aren't there yet," he said, continuing their walk. "But it is an ideal place for just that." He took her by the hand. "I'm going to ask you a question, and I hope you trust me enough to answer. You told me another man let you down. Did he harm you?"

She looked away.

"Let me in, Darcie."

She cried as he whispered to her. His whispers were for consoling the wounded woman, not for the one holding a secret. She never thought she could be both. She had always considered herself a terrible liar. It turns out she was better than she thought. She despised herself for it. How had it gone this far? This wasn't her.

She decided to tell him and accept the consequences of her actions. If he never wanted to see her again, then it was nothing less than she deserved. If she had been honest to begin with, she wouldn't be in this mess. Maybe he would understand, perhaps not, but it was too late for that now.

With her thoughts raging and Connor's voice echoing in her ear, she could hardly concentrate. She closed her eyes tight, wringing her hands. She wanted to scream for silence. All she needed was quiet so she could get her thoughts together and confess. She dropped to the ground and rocked back and forth, hugging her knees.

Connor watched as she closed herself off. She wasn't listening to him; she was listening to God only knew what narrative in her head. Whatever it was, it wasn't helping. She wouldn't stop crying, and she looked like she would go into shock. He had to put a stop to it, and his whispers were not helping like they always did.

Suddenly, her voice rose through angry tears. "I didn't try to stop him! I didn't fight back! I didn't even scream!"

A sick feeling crept into Connor's stomach. He tried to hold her, but she pushed him away.

"I'm a weakling! A stupid woman who didn't see it coming and now look at me! I see my own shadow and jump. How I got to Ireland on my own is beyond me. The only thing that kept me standing was my own sheer will, and that was hanging by a thread! I've been afraid for ten years. Ten years, Connor!"

Connor began to speak.

She interrupted. "And now that monster shows up here!"

Someone did harm her. She had been raped. And the man who did it had been at Grace's cafe. Connor wanted to throw up. He had a hundred questions, but now was not the time.

She opened her eyes, the rocking stopped. She looked directly at him. "Connor." She sniffled and shook a little. "I'm sorry. I should have told you. I wasn't honest. You were everything, and then I couldn't tell you. I wouldn't tell. Do you still want me? You want this shell? This pathetic creature?"

For Connor, listening to Darcie apologize for not telling him was torture. She didn't owe him anything. She could have kept that secret and had every right to, so far as he was concerned. He wanted to murder the man for what he did. A broken nose and prison weren't enough. But he would deal with that later.

Connor gathered her onto his lap. He cried with her. He cried for her. They cried until they were both spent.

"What can I do to help you?" he asked.

A weak smile emerged. "Do? Don't you know? You already did it." She threw her arms around his neck, nearly bowling him over. "I'm not afraid when I'm with you. I'm happier than I have been in a long time. I didn't come here looking for anyone, but I found you."

He placed his lips to her forehead. "You're stronger than you think. My brave Irish girl."

He wouldn't ask any more questions. Later, they would deal with finding the man and making sure he was no longer a threat. For the moment, it was enough that she was safe with Connor.

IT WAS some time before they resumed their walk. Darcie often stopped to admire the landscape and pick a few wild flowers.

"It really is beautiful here, isn't it?" she said, watching a magpie fly overhead. "There's something about it that grabs all the senses and demands admiration. Even the air is laced with some kind of magic that seeps into your soul."

Connor was pleased. He knew she would like it here. "Aye, I have to agree with you on that. There is no place on earth like home."

Home, she thought. Home. Her heart began to crack. "When are we—"

Her speech abruptly halted as she gaped. She had dreamed of it so many times, she recognized it in an instant. The church from her dreams. Sometimes it felt like she wasn't herself in the dream. Darcie wasn't even sure she believed in God. Not anymore. But never the less, she had that reoccurring dream and now it was staring her in the face.

"You don't like it. I'm sorry, love. I dragged you out here for nothing."

Darcie came to and realized she hadn't heard a word Connor has said. "I'm sorry. I got lost in my thoughts. What did you say?"

"I asked what you thought of this place, and you said nothing."

"I'm sorry, I was surprised. You wouldn't even know it was here. It's hidden perfectly behind this hill. Can we go inside?" she said, hoping to sound enthusiastic.

When she asked him before about old churches, she had never thought he would find the one. They approached the small church, and Darcie laid her hand on the door to push it open, but hesitated.

Connor took an old, heavy key from his pocket and unlocked the door. "We can sit awhile in here and take a rest."

He led her inside and sat down on a stone bench in front of the altar. Her pulse thundered. She could feel something pressing on her, a presence.

"They say this church is four hundred years old. But it's not what it seems."

Darcie watched Connor as he told the story.

"You see, the altar? There's no cross on it. There are no crosses anywhere in here."

She looked around. In her dreams, she had never noticed there were no crosses.

"It's a fake. But some argue that nothing is more holy than love."

As his musical words hypnotized her mind, hazy images began to appear. The air around her grew thick, heavy with voices and obscured sounds. It was apparent Connor did not hear them, so she said nothing.

"This was built by a man for the woman he loved. They couldn't be together because she was forced into an arranged marriage. He built this as a place of refuge and as a lasting sign of his devotion to her. It's said that they used to meet here in secret until one day she didn't come."

On the altar appeared the hazy image of a man and woman entwined. Their shadows flickered on the wall through candlelight.

"She had disappeared. No one knew where she went. She was never seen again."

Darcie's head was heavy on her shoulders. She stared, disbelieving, at the scene playing out before her and spoke low like a voyeur attempting not to be caught.

She tucked herself closer to Connor's side. "That's grim. They really never knew what happened to her?"

"Some said she killed herself because her husband was cruel and the only way to be free of him was death."

Even as he said it, Darcie knew that was not what happened. She heard crying. Then she heard a woman say "forgive me."

She tried not to gulp. It was overwhelming, and she grew scared and confused.

As Connor went on, the faded, distant voices grew louder. The impossible ghostly sounds and scenes were inexplicable. Maybe she was finally losing her mind. The stress had won the battle, and she was slipping into madness. *I can't tell him all this. I don't even understand it myself. It's insanity.*

Connor put his arm around her shoulders as if he'd

heard her cry for help. She wanted to crawl onto his lap and hide. Maybe he could keep these ghosts away.

He continued the story. "Some say her husband murdered her for her betrayal. Others said she fell pregnant with her lover's baby and left so she could keep that one part of her true love safe."

"That's very sad," is all Darcie could say. "To be forced to leave the one you love."

The man and woman disappeared. She sat, staring at the faded carvings on the altar. She felt the ache of their loss and began to wonder how she would feel if she had to leave Connor. *You fool, you already know that it would break your heart and his. He deserves better.*

She got down on her knees, looking closely at the carvings on the altar. Her eyes got huge, her face pale. She pointed to the Celtic knot in the center of the altar. It was identical to her necklace.

"What are the odds of that?" Even Connor had to admit it was a spooky coincidence.

Fate. If she could scream in its face, she would. All she wanted was peace and to leave the past behind, but it hadn't stayed there where it belonged. She had tried to outrun it, come halfway across the world, and it still hunted her down. And now, to top it off, she was seeing and hearing ghosts. Even her beautiful present wasn't sacred. She couldn't begin to comprehend everything.

He watched her try to make sense of it. She was delving deeper into a place in her mind where he couldn't follow. He circled his hand on her back. This place was supposed to make her happy, not upset her. His plan was failing. He needed to get her out of her head and into his arms.

Softer than a prayer, she said his name. Without a word, he brought her into his arms. She wanted to lose herself. It was all too much. She whispered into his ear as he pulled her onto his lap. He would protect her from whatever was coming.

"Connor, I need you."

She looked so fragile in that moment. She had never asked again after the night inside the ruins. He wasn't about to refuse her. Nothing is more holy than true love, he'd said. He would sacrifice everything for her. How could anyone want to hurt this precious woman he loved? And how could she bear it all?

"I'm afraid."

He framed her cheeks in his hands as she burrowed her face into his palm. Her lips tasted of their shared salty tears. "No one will harm you again. Not while I'm here."

She couldn't get close enough to him as she fit herself snug in his lap. *Fill me up, heal the pain, find me.* "Please, don't let me go."

"Never."

CHAPTER 27

"*Did you get the letter to Michael?*" *Anne asked Maude, her trusted ladies' maid.*

"*I surely did, mistress,*" *said Maude.* "*He did not give me a reply.*"

Anne looked out the window at the snowcapped mountains and felt the faintest chill in the breeze wafting through the open window. "*He is thinking up a plan, no doubt.*"

Anne Malloy waited three days to hear from her lover. She had written to him to say she was pregnant and planned to run away. She had not shared her husband's bed in months. There would be no doubt of her infidelity. He was cruel on the best of days and would surely murder her for her betrayal. She had to protect her unborn child. She didn't want to leave without telling Michael, but his silence was making her uneasy.

She couldn't hold off leaving any longer. Her husband was away and would be returning soon. Her window of opportunity to escape safely was nearly closed.

She wrote Michael a second letter and sent Maude to

deliver it. Still no reply. Anne had to leave. She thought Michael loved her, but it was apparent by his silence she had misjudged him.

Anne waited for the cover of night, and with Maude's help, she escaped without being seen by anyone. She made only one stop before leaving forever—her church. Once inside, she fell to her knees in front of the altar and cried. "Forgive me," was all she said.

Little did Anne know Maude had never delivered the letters. In fact, Maude had taken great lengths to make sure her mistress left and never returned. She wanted her permanently out of the way. She had thought about poisoning Anne, but she didn't have the courage.

"The filthy slut sleeping with another man when she has a perfectly wonderful husband who is handsome and rich," Maude said to herself.

Master had smiled at Maude a few times and invited her to his bed. Mistress didn't do her duties, so of course, he would find comfort elsewhere. Maude could make him happy. Mistress could not. Better for her to leave.

When Michael asked Maude where Anne had gone, and why, she feigned ignorance of the whole business. Of course, there would be talk in the village, but that would die down, and then she and Master would be free to marry. Anne didn't deserve him. Maude did. Good riddance to the slut and her bastard.

"TELL HIM THE TRUTH. You can have it all if you tell him. It is all here within your grasp," a voice said to Darcie.

141

The ghostly face of Anne Malloy appeared over Connor's shoulder. "You are safe and loved here in my place, our place. It was built out of love, and you insult it by denying the truth. Stop holding back. Tell him now."

Darcie saw the spirits again. They were just as she was with Connor in that passionate moment.

Darcie shut her eyes tight. Something within her had broken free or taken over. Connor wasn't sure which.

"Look at me," Connor pleaded.

She looked at him with round, dark eyes.

"Acushla, it's time to let go. It's only us here. Let it all out," he urged.

Time to let it all go, he'd said. She did. She tipped her face to the sun, releasing a scream that should have cracked the sky; purging her fear, pain, anger, sadness, agony and guilt, leaving behind a gaping hole where the darkness had burrowed in her soul.

He held her while she wailed, telling her she would never be alone again. He would not abandon her. Stand or fall, it would be together for always.

"Let me find you."

Darcie kept her eyes on him and surrendered. Connor smiled when she released a long, sweet sigh. Her eyes became light, dreamy, and happy.

There was no use denying or withholding the truth anymore. She took in a long breath and would swear she smelled burning candle wax.

"Connor, I love you."

The three words he'd been waiting to hear. "And I love you," he said as he swiped her hair from her face.

The clouds in the sky split the sun into rays, beaming

heavenly light in every direction. It lit her auburn hair like a radiant sunrise. And as she slowly exhaled, he felt her blossom. He could feel the sunlight she had taken in pulsing back to him. It was like seeing a rose bloom, and he caressed every soft petal. He found her.

She was spent and barely had a drop of strength. With her face turned into his neck, she murmured, "You found me. I'm yours. God help me, I'm yours."

———

THEY STAYED on the altar in each other's arms for a long while. The warm sun was soon covered by a cloud.

"You're getting cold. We had best get you clothed before you catch your death." Grabbing her bottom, he swung his legs over the edge of the stone.

She giggled, squirming.

"Don't be saying you're looking for more. I think you nearly killed me, woman."

She laughed, crawled out of his lap, and almost fell to the ground. She hadn't realized that her limbs were a pair of anchors.

He caught her. "Let me dress you."

She sat on the stone bench while he tended to her. "I should have told you earlier. This is going to sound strange, but this church, I've been dreaming about it for a long time."

"Is that so?" he asked, as if what she had just said was completely normal. "Was I in your dreams as well?" he asked in a devilish voice.

She laughed. "No, I was always alone, kneeling at the

altar. In every dream, I always said the same thing—forgive me."

"Well, it's no wonder you be asking forgiveness for what we just did on that altar. I think we made the angels blush."

Her cheeks turned red.

"It's a little late for you to be blushing now. Your secret is out. You've an animal under your skin."

Her face went a deeper red when Connor winked his twinkling blue eye.

"In all seriousness, though, you dream of this church?" He was putting on her socks and wellies.

"Yes, quite a lot. I didn't know it was a real place until you brought me here."

"So that is why you looked like you'd seen a ghost when you saw the place. I see." He stood and dressed. "Tell me more about these dreams."

"Well, I would enter the church. There was a sense of sadness and joy at the same time. I would run my hands over the carvings in the walls and on the altar, trying to figure out what they were. That story you told me about the church being built for a woman. I think that's my final piece of the puzzle. In my dreams, it was me in the church, and sometimes it was me but not me. Does that make sense?"

"I think I get your meaning. Go on."

"Well, today when we ... "

"Made passionate love on a pagan altar where you turned into a ravenous animal, had countless orgasms, and still begged me for more?" He looked at her matter-of-factly.

Her mouth dropped open.

"You're not going to deny it, are you?"

She looked around her with a grin.

"Ah-ha! There she is! The cat that ate all the cream. Come here, you." He brought her into his stride with his arm around her shoulders as they started to leave.

She was looking at the carvings on the wall and stopped. "This carving. I could never make out what it was. But I see now." She ran her hand over the fading markings, etching them into her mind's eye.

"Darcie, that looks like us."

"It does." Shivers ran down her spine. The picture she traced was of a naked man and woman. She was sitting on his lap. They had their arms and legs wrapped around each other in an intimate moment. "I know what you're going to say. Don't use the F word," she said. She'd had enough of fate for one day.

"I don't need to say the F word. I just did it to you— thoroughly!"

She clapped her hand over his mouth.

"It's only now that you're feeling shy?" he chuckled. "If anyone were within a mile, they would have heard you howling. So, me talking about it isn't going to change that." He led her outside. "Go on then, tell me the rest. Where did you go when we were together in there? I spoke to you, and it was like you weren't there."

"You're right. I was someplace else. I know this will sound insane, but that woman, the one the church was built for, I saw her. She came to me while we were together. I know what happened to her. She showed me." She waited for Connor to dismiss her, but he didn't. "In my dream, when it was me but not me, it's her. She found out she was pregnant with her lover's baby. Her husband was a cruel man, and she wanted to keep her child safe. She decided the best choice was to run away. Her lover never knew about the baby. It was her asking for forgiveness for leaving and taking their unborn child. I saw it all like it was a movie playing before my eyes. I heard a woman's voice and a child laughing in the distance."

"Well, that's that mystery solved."

"You're serious? You're not going to say I'm crazy or I don't know, call me a witch or something?"

"There are all sorts of things I don't understand, Darcie. But I do have a good understanding of you. Today, I possessed your body, but something else had possession of your mind. So, if you tell me the spirit of that woman visited you, then I believe you. Plain and simple."

"Damn Irish!"

His eyebrows shot up. She never swore or got angry.

"Do all of you just accept this mystical ... " She didn't want to finish the sentence with the word she was thinking.

"Stuff?"

She scowled at him.

"I'll remind you that you're one of us. Not all of us get visits from spirits and hear the land speaking, but we generally don't write off those who do!" he scolded.

"You're right. I'm sorry. I had no right to be so insulting." Ashamed of herself, she looked at the ground.

"Love, listen to me."

She still looked at the ground.

"Darcie, look at me, so I know you're with me," he ordered. She was in for an earful. "There has hardly been a night I don't find you having a nightmare. You cry, shake and scream. The first night you were crying and saying, forgive me. That's what you usually say. But it scares the hell out of me some nights when you scream for help and shake with fear. I didn't know what to do. I pulled you closer to me so I could make you feel safe. It worked. You settled down and slept like a babe. That's what I've done every time.

Now you're telling me that this church is the one in that nightmare. You tell me that the spirit of the woman in my story is speaking to you. You didn't know this place existed; you'd never heard the story. So why would I doubt you? You're many things. A liar isn't one of them.

You never told me about your dreams, and yet I bring you here. I even chose a necklace for you that has the exact knot that is on that altar. This is private land. I got permission to bring you here because I thought it was a place that would speak to you. And it did. If I had known about the dream I would have handled it differently. But you have a tether to this place."

He paused to catch his breath. "Well, if that isn't FATE, then I don't know what is!" He went to take a step forward but changed his mind. "And another thing—and you better be listening good! You're meant to be with me. I've been waiting for you, and if you think for a moment, I'll let you go, you are mistaken. True love happens so rarely. Some would call it love at first sight. I never believed in that. At least not until I met you."

Her joyous tears flowed freely. "You really love me?"

He'd spoken his piece and was now calm. "You know I do," he said softly.

"Yes."

"And?"

A breeze circled her at that moment and she blurted, "I love you too!"

He smiled in triumph.

"When I saw you in the hall, I tried to tell myself I was attracted to you because you're—"

"Handsome and charming?" He was enjoying her revelation.

"Yes!" She was exasperated. "I've loved you since the beginning. I was too scared to say it. That's what your mother was saying to me. She said you love me."

"Mum is too smart for her own good. You make me happy. Very happy."

"You make me," she exhaled hard, "exhausted."

"Exhausted, is it?"

"What we have ... I've never had anything like this before. And yes, it's exhausting. I think about you day and night. I think about you while I shampoo my hair, when I'm in bed, shopping, watching TV, eating, you name it! It's constantly you, you, you. I had given up a long time ago. I didn't expect to come here and find the piece of me that's been missing. You make me whole, you make me feel safe, and you make me happier than I've ever been."

"See, how hard was that?" he said, making her laugh. "I love you, you love me, and we have bleeding deadly sex. There, we said it. Now, can we go and enjoy each other?"

"Yes." She beamed him a sexy grin as her eyes went a little dark.

"Whoa, lass! As much as I like that animal we released, I can't tame that beast anymore today."

"Not even a little?"

She moved to his mouth greedily and bit his bottom lip. He grabbed her arms, plopping her a foot away, and stared her down and with a growl. She took off running up the footpath.

He caught her up against the car and kissed her senseless. "That animal needs to stay caged the rest of the day."

"I promise it will. Oops, I was crossing my fingers!"

"Darcie Hartwell, you're a fiend! You are!"

"Only when it comes to you, my love."

His mouth dropped open.

"I like it when I shock you, O'Brian."

"You're going to be the death of me. But I can't think of any better way to go. I'm famished. Dinner?"

She jumped into his arms and went for his neck to gobble him up.

"I'll take that as a yes!"

CHAPTER 28

IT WAS EARLY in the morning. Darcie couldn't sleep and didn't want to wake Connor. He'd been taking such good care of her the past couple of days. She knew he was worried, and it was taking a toll on him. The body of an American man being pulled from Swan Lake was being shown on the news. She watched the story play out with wide eyes. She stared without blinking, not saying a word. Holding her breath.

It was him. She couldn't believe it. He was dead.

She exhaled, took the remote, and shut off the television. She didn't care why or how. Good riddance to him. She was free.

AFTER GIVING a statement to the police and reliving her horror story, Darcie was fit to be tied and run down. The police gave no details of the man's death. She didn't want to know. All she cared about was that he was dead and gone.

Henry and Sylvia suggested that Connor bring her to their house for a few days. It would give them all a chance to understand each other better while providing Connor and Darcie the opportunity to rest.

Sylvia met them at the door with a smile and a hug for them both. Henry was putting the kettle on and feeding Molly when they entered the kitchen.

"Come here, lass," Henry said to Darcie as he pulled her into a warm bear hug. He choked on his tears, rocking her in his arms. "You're home now." He reached for Connor, bringing him into the fold. "You're both home now." Molly jumped up Darcie's leg, begging for attention, offering some relief from the emotional moment. "Now, you two get settled and tea will be ready soon. Darcie, I have a special treat for you. I went to Skelligs Chocolate today."

Henry handed her a robins-egg blue cylinder of chocolate truffles. Before she could thank him, he raised his hand to silence her and shuffled the pair of them out of the kitchen to unpack while he made tea.

Sylvia waited for Connor and Darcie to be out of earshot. "Is that where you disappeared to today? You old softy. And nothing for your wife, I suppose?"

Henry opened the bread box and presented her with her own blue cylinder. Molly danced around, wanting to know where her present was. Henry ignored her while he enjoyed a stolen moment with his wife.

"I KNOW you usually prefer to be on top, but would you like the bottom?" asked Connor.

Darcie clapped her hand over his grinning mouth. "Shhh!" She closed the bedroom door. "You may not care who hears, but I would prefer your parents not know about that ... "

"Stuff?"

She laughed. The bunk bed of Connor's childhood sat in the corner of the room, draped in a welcoming red plaid.

"There's a sound I haven't heard in a couple days," he said.

"I feel better already just being here. Are you sure I shouldn't sleep in the guest room?"

"Absolutely not. You want to be apart?"

"No," she said, hugging his waist.

"Me neither. My parents aren't strict Catholics. Besides, they adore you. You could have your way with me on the kitchen table during tea time. All they would do is move their cups out of the way."

They both laughed. Henry and Sylvia heard their laughter from the next room and smiled.

"The other bed isn't big enough for the two of us and Molly. If I know her, she will sneak into bed with you."

Darcie smiled at the comforting thought of snuggling with the soft terrier.

Connor was right. The next morning, Darcie had more red hair than she went to sleep with. She and Molly were bundled, sweet as you please, sound asleep. Molly was snoring into Darcie's hair, blowing it in and away from her nostrils with every breath. Darcie had a soft smile on her lips.

We'll be needing to get you a dog, acushla.

No QUESTIONS WERE ASKED. Now was a time for moving forward, not looking to the past. The quiet days were spent doing nothing in particular. Walking the green fields, always with Molly tagging along, visiting places along the Ring of Kerry, resting on the beach, and taking in the sea air.

Connor never left Darcie's side, and she was grateful for the support from Henry and Sylvia. They felt like her family, and just as Henry had said, Darcie was home.

Each night, the four of them sat together each with a whiskey in hand. Darcie would curl under Connor's arm, with Molly on her lap, listening to Henry and Sylvia telling stories. Connor, of course, hated it and groaned with every embarrassing tale and photograph Sylvia showed Darcie.

SYLVIA WAS STANDING in front of her kitchen window, staring outside. Henry slid his arm around her waist and peered over her head. Connor and Darcie were asleep in the hammock.

"You're thinking how can someone who has suffered as our Darcie has be so lovely? And how can we help Connor to help her'?"

"If she were my daughter ... "

"She's as good as."

Sylvia rested her head against Henry. "When did you get so smart, you old goat?"

"Was I right then? Lucky guess."

"I like her Henry. More importantly, Connor loves her. She's the one he's been waiting for."

"Aye she is. She's part of our family now. We will take care of her. Anyone she has in America won't help her. We will. I wonder what her mother is thinking. I hope she's ashamed of herself."

"Connor said she left home. He didn't say her mother disowned her."

"No, but that's what happened, mark my words. What sort of mother does that? Good thing Darcie has you now."

"And you."

CHAPTER 29

DARCIE WALKED DOWN THE STAIRCASE, foregoing the elevator. For the first time in her life, she felt like making an entrance. In black satin heels, wearing a new blue dress that flared just below her knee and hit her curves in all the right places, she descended the stairs with style and confidence. Tonight, she and Connor were starting fresh, and to celebrate, they were going to the new swanky restaurant in town.

The blonde behind the front desk saw her first. "Wow, she's changed."

"Who?" Asked the hotel manager before he spotted Darcie and found himself gawking.

Shamus felt the manager's elbow in his side and looked up. He, too, found himself gaping. *This poor lass has been through so much since she arrived. One would think it would break her. But no. Look at her, she's radiant.*

Shamus met her at the bottom step, took her hand, and escorted her across the room to the front door. "Well, aren't you a picture lass! Give us a twirl." He held out his arm and twirled her as if they were dancing. "I hope you don't mind an old man saying this, but your smile lights up this whole room. A woman in love is the most beautiful sight in this world, I say. Connor pulled up as you came down the stairs. You'll knock him dead looking like that." He winked as he opened the door for her.

"Thank you, Shamus." She kissed his cheek as she danced out the door.

Connor whistled as she exited the hotel. "I saw Shamus giving you a twirl. I can see why."

She flashed a smile.

"Come on then. Give us a spin so I can get a good look at you." She gave him a turn. Connor fell backward onto the car. "You're a knockout!"

"Thank you. No one ever called me that before."

"I'll be changing that. Now, get in the car before I tear that pretty dress off of you and forget all about dinner."

THEY ARRIVED at the new restaurant Merlot anticipating an exceptional evening. That balloon popped the moment they stepped inside the door. The place was decorated in a modern decor of black, white, and gray. The artwork, and they would use that term loosely, was nothing but solitary, large, white circles on a black canvas. Why bother? The floors were slate gray tile, the seats and tables were all stainless steel. Slim straight lines, no fuss, and no color were the order of the day.

All in all, the restaurant looked like a mortician's office.

Darcie nearly yelped when she sat on her stainless-steel seat. It was freezing!

Connor looked at the menu and frowned. The wine menu had about one-hundred choices. The dinner menu had three. Darcie sat looking over the absurd menu and didn't have the heart to look at Connor. He would know she didn't like the place. This was supposed to mark a new beginning for them, and she wanted everything to be perfect. She was concentrating on putting on a fake smile when Connor leaned across the table.

"What morbid eejit designed this place? I feel like I should be a body on a slab waiting for an autopsy." She burst out laughing, making a scene and making him laugh as well. "You want to get out of here?"

"I thought you'd never ask!"

They were still laughing when a woman's voice rudely interrupted. Suddenly, Connor did look like a body waiting for an autopsy. His back straightened, his grip on Darcie's hand tightened enough to make her wince.

A slim, tall, peroxide blonde wearing enough dark eye makeup to make one wonder what she was covering up, bright red lipstick that even a clown would have turned down, and a black dress that left absolutely nothing to the imagination except to wonder how she got it on, was standing by their table. Darcie swore the woman's tongue forked at the tip. And she marveled at how she could have survived being rolled over by a tractor-trailer because surely that was the only way she got that cheap, rubber scrap of a dress adhered to herself. And judging by the crushing grip Connor had on her hand, the woman needed no introduction.

"Kristina." His jaw went rigid, his voice acid.

Sweet as spiked punch, Kristina leaned down and tried to kiss his mouth. He pushed her away before she even got close. On the upside, at least Darcie now knew he hadn't broken one of her hands.

"Oh, come on, Con, don't be like that. You can't still be mad at me?"

Darcie doesn't need this. I don't need this. This was supposed to be a special evening. Keep away, you viper! Connor looked at Darcie with apologetic eyes.

"Oh! I am so sorry! Are you on a date?" Kristina turned to look down at Darcie with a bright red, condescending smirk. "I didn't notice you." She turned back to Connor after her quick dismissal of Darcie. "Aren't you going to introduce me?"

"No," he said sternly and escorted Darcie out of the restaurant, practically dragging her. He couldn't get them out of there fast enough.

Once outside in the air, Connor took a moment to breathe. *Of all the people to show up, it had to be Kristina. And to show up now? After everything that's happened? Impeccable timing, as always. Just as things are getting better, will we ever get a moment's peace? Darcie, how will she handle this? Should I take her home?*

He wasn't sure what to do. All he knew was that in his entire life, he had never been so furious. Darcie solved part of his problem by taking the lead. "Fish and chips?" she asked, breaking the heavy silence.

"I love you," he said with relief.

CHAPTER 30

EATING THEIR FISH AND CHIPS, they sat in silence while parked on the side of the street. A summer storm was beginning to kick up its heels. The wind was starting to rush, and the rain began to fall. Darcie watched the people on the sidewalk take out their umbrellas.

A man passed by with his dog that reminded her of Henry and Molly. He was dressed in an Irish cap and light jacket, holding a black umbrella; he had a friendly face. She watched the man in the rearview mirror as he went inside a nearby door.

He must live in the upstairs apartment over the shop. I wonder if he has anyone waiting for him. I hope so.

The raindrops' sound on the car roof grew louder and louder as it streamed down the windows, now making it impossible for her to see anything outside clearly. The street lights looked like a kaleidoscope through the running water.

Connor barely touched his food while staring out the windshield at nothing in particular. He was brooding. In the distance, thunder and lightning clashed. The storm mimicked his foul, conflicted mood.

The silence was making Darcie uncomfortable. Connor had been gnawing on the same chip for minutes and probably didn't know it. She hated that Kristina had done this to him. She had to do something.

"I'm going to address the elephant in the room," she said. Connor put down his partially eaten chip. "That was your ex-fiancé?"

"Yes."

"It was the first time you've seen her since she left?"

"Yes, and I could have been happy the rest of my days not seeing her again. You don't think I'm upset because I miss her, do you? Because I don't."

"No. I know you better than that." She could tell he was sincere, so she decided to drop the subject and then quickly changed her mind. For once, she had to speak, and this time she really let it rip. "Well, if you ask me, she looks like a bony ass, bleach blonde brasser who needs to lay off the hairspray, take at least three layers of that clown makeup off and try wearing a dress that doesn't look like it came from an auto parts store. And she can take her prissy attitude and shove it in her hole!"

Connor's eyebrows went up in delighted surprise. "I've never heard you insult anyone like that, and well done on our vernacular!" She'd hit that nail on the head and said what he couldn't. "Is that what it takes to get your Irish up? Worrying over me?"

Her Irish was up alright! "I don't like insulting people, but sometimes people just deserve it. She was begging for it! I don't know what you saw in her. She's got dragon tramp stamped on her forehead," she said flatly.

Connor broke into a belly laugh. Darcie didn't see what was so funny. She sat with her hands crossed on her lap and blinked.

"You're right. Looking back, I don't know what I saw in her. I can't think of one good thing to say. After she left, I was angry. But it didn't take long for me to realize I was angry with myself, not her. She did me a favor by leaving, and that's the truth of it." He put down his bundle of food and turned in his seat to face her. "I wish I had met you all those years ago. We would have had more time together."

He had wanted to ask her in a romantic setting, but at that moment, he was desperate and couldn't wait any longer. If he had learned anything from the past few days, it's that they are better together. The need for Darcie permanently by his side was more urgent than choosing the perfect time and place.

"Please say you will stay."

"What?" She put her bundle of food on the dashboard.

"Stay. Make a life with me. I can't be without you, and I can't go on not knowing for sure you're not going to leave. You don't have to give me an answer right now. I know I'm asking a lot, but think about it."

Darcie had thought about him saying it. He had said he loves her and hinted about her staying, but there was no official talk about making a life together. She had dreamed of the life they could have. It was her favorite dream. She couldn't help but think about how everything was nearly stolen from her just days ago. It was Connor who pulled her through.

Connor watched her. He was trying to figure out what she was thinking, but her face, for once, was blank. She stayed quiet another minute. He began to kick himself.

"Love, I'm sorry. I shouldn't have said it."

"You didn't mean it?"

He ran his hand through his hair in frustration. "Aye, I meant it."

"Really?"

Hope came across his face. "Aye. I love you, Darcie. I said I would wait for you, and I meant it. But that doesn't mean I want to wait."

Her eyes welled up with tears.

He braced himself for the worst.

"That's good, because I don't want to keep you waiting."

His head snapped up, and she smiled. He dove across the seat. "And for a minute there, I thought you were going to break my heart!"

Before she could respond, he took her under a furious kiss laced with anger and hurt. All the bad memories of his past relationship bubbled to the surface while all the previous days' pain and stress came flooding out. There was something urgent, desperate in his kisses.

"Connor?" she gulped.

"Yes," he said, not wanting to break away, "my love?" He was trying to eat her whole.

She tore her mouth away, giving him her neck to feast on. She inhaled sharply when he did the one thing he had sworn to himself never to do.

He stopped his assault. He was breathing heavily into her neck, where a bruise was already showing. "I'm sorry.

Sometimes, it isn't easy to be gentle when I want you so badly."

Connor needed to lose himself, and she knew it. He had a fierce and violent urge. It was thrilling for Darcie to realize she was going to set that loose.

"Still want to take this dress off of me?"

"You have no idea what I want to do to you." His eyes turned to smoke. His voice threatening a delicious warning.

She dared him. "Show me."

———

THEY ARRIVED HOME, and before the car was in park, Darcie jumped out. "Catch me, O'Brian, and you can have me."

She ran through the heavy rain to the backyard. He went after her like an animal hunting its prey. Except for the flashes of lightning that lit up the night, he could see nothing. He stopped and looked around, calling her name. When he got close enough, she stepped into his line of sight as a crack of lightning lit up the dark.

His breath stopped at the sight of her.

She was under the porch roof, standing in her black high heels, wearing nothing but black lace that, thank the saints, left little to the imagination. Her blue dress pooled at her feet; her long hair stuck over her shoulders, dripping rain over her breast. Her beautiful eyes were as dark as the lace she touted.

He took long, fast strides toward his siren. She found it arousing to know she had all the power here in this moment. He was mad with greed, but she knew what she wanted. Moreover, she knew what he needed.

She raised her hand, halting his advance.

He stopped dead in his tracks.

"Don't hold back. Be whatever you want. Take whatever you want," she said.

And he did.

Connor was drenched. His muscles showed through the white-soaked cotton as it clung to him like a second skin so pale and transparent.

His eyes gleamed sex. She forcefully tugged him closer by his belt and pressed herself against him.

He dragged his thumb over her mouth, parting her lips. She kissed his fingertip and bit it. Any control Connor had left snapped. The blood in his ears roared. He needed to taste her. His teeth scraped against the triangle of lace between her thighs.

"How do you feel about this pair?" he growled.

"Never liked them."

One tear, and they were gone. Darcie, his life's blood, tasted sweet and was so hot, Connor wondered why the lace hadn't merely disintegrated. Once he had his fill, and she was trembling, he lapped the rainwater on her skin.

"Here. Now," she demanded as she tore open his shirt. "Fair's fair, O'Brian." She smiled at his shocked face.

He had said she was full of surprises. He was about to find out another.

Connor was wild, his hands were everywhere. He thrust, sucked, licked, and bit while he took her there against the door.

Darcie reveled in every moment and gave back all she

got. All around them, thunder and lightning clashed. The smell of ozone mixed with the salty sea and flowers' scent was intoxicating.

Together they came strongly.

He was nowhere near through with her, which was good because she wasn't finished with him.

He swung her up in his arms and carried her inside. She flipped a switch with her foot, igniting the fireplace, casting its flame and heat on the walls. If ever there was a place to burn, it was here together.

He bent her over the sofa and took her hard.

"Oh, God!" she shouted.

"Let's leave him out of it tonight. I'm surely going to Hell for the mark I left on your neck." He looked down. "And for the one on your perfect bum."

She barked orders, and he obeyed.

It was frantic, rough, hot, greedy, primitive. All he wanted was more and more each time she screamed, cried out, and shuddered his name again and again.

She came once, twice. She crashed so hard into a peak her ears rang, and with the third dragged him with her over the edge of the world.

HE COLLAPSED ONTO HER BACK. He was going to need a minute. A day would be better. A week would be perfect. In fact, why not just retire now?

Darcie hung limply over the sofa, like wet laundry on a line. Trembling and sweating, like the thoroughly ravished woman she was.

"Connor." She blew her hair out of her eyes with a puff. Their profane shadow was dancing on the wall in the flickering flames.

"I know we can't stay like this." His chest was heaving while he admired how the fire reflected off the beads of sweat on her back. "I need a minute. Then I will carry you to bed."

"You don't have to."

He cradled her weak body in his arms. "You let me take you with no less finesse and tenderness than a wild dog. Yes, I do need to carry you."

Even though Darcie had wanted it, Connor needed her to remember she was precious and his to protect and treasure. He handled her with the greatest care as he laid her comfortably in bed with her head resting on her fluffy pillow and tucked her under the soft duvet.

Connor collapsed in bed, speechless and stunned by his actions. Darcie was exhausted, spent, and reveling in it all. She hadn't known that side of herself existed, but now that she did, she would bring it out more often.

Outside, the storm had calmed into a light rain.

"I want to do that again," she said.

"Jesus, she's gone rogue on me," he said with weary astonishment. "What's come over you letting me have my way with you like that?"

"Who said it was your way?"

His jaw dropped open. "Where is my sweet, submissive girl?"

"I gave her the night off."

He chuckled and brought her under his arm. "I always knew you would be a wonderful terror."

She liked the sound of that. "Sondra was right."

"About what?"

"When I was ready to wear that blue dress, she said that I would be ready to wear the black lace."

He choked on his ragged breath. "Your Sondra is surely the gatekeeper to sin." He kissed Darcie on the nose. "I'll send her some chocolates."

They lay together, listening to the gentle rain. Connor began drifting off to sleep. There was one thing left for Darcie to say before he was deaf to the world.

"I love you, Connor O'Brian, and you are mine."

CHAPTER 31

"Darcie!" Sondra shouted as she saw her walk inside her shop.

"Hi, Sondra!"

"I've been thinking about you."

Sondra gave Darcie a big hug, then stepped back, looking her over. What she expected to see and what was standing before her were two different things. After the past few days' trauma, Sondra thought Darcie would be a helpless wreck, and she didn't blame her for a second. What an awful thing to happen to her dear friend. The thought of someone harming Darcie made her so angry she could spit. It all made sense now why Darcie had been so shy and innocent when they met. She had lived in fear too long and was traumatized.

But the woman standing in her shop now—no one would ever guess she had ever been anything but deliriously happy in life. Sondra proudly took a little personal credit for being part of the beautiful transformation, but knew who deserved most of the credit. Since there was obviously no crisis to avert, Sondra decided to keep things light.

"You're glowing! Connor's that good, huh?"

"Sondra!" Darcie blushed.

"You can't fool me. Besides, your eyes betray you and judging by the shade of your cheeks, I say we skip the tea and go straight for the whiskey. That's a gorgeous necklace you're wearing, by the way." She turned the store sign to closed, flipped the lock, and hurried to the kitchen.

"So, where do you want to start? The hot sex or the steamy hot sex?" Sondra teased.

Darcie was grateful for Sondra's ability to read a situation and know when to let dead dogs lie. She had left the pain in the past and had no desire to dredge it up. "You don't hold anything back, do you?"

"Life is too short to beat around the bush," Sondra said, flicking her hand in the air. She poured two glasses of whiskey and placed them on the table. "Sooo? Last time you were here, you and Connor had gotten down and dirty inside the ruins and saw stars in each other's eyes. Still seeing stars?"

"Yes." She was gushing. "Sondra, I don't even know where to begin." She sipped her whiskey. "Everything seems to have moved so fast, and yet it feels like I've known him my whole life. He says that we are fated to be together. I never believed in all that, but I love him."

"Love! Fate! What a way for a story to begin!" She swooned and drank her whiskey. "No wonder you two hit it off so fast." Sondra grabbed a box of chocolates from the counter. "Thank Connor for me, will you?" She popped a truffle in her mouth and offered the box to Darcie.

"It's like I fell into a life that was already mine. It was waiting for me to come find it." She took a bite of chocolate. "He took me to meet his parents."

"And?"

"They couldn't have been nicer." Darcie went on to talk about Connor asking her to make a life with him.

"So, when is the wedding?"

Darcie laughed. "Slow down. I have to catch my breath. But he does have a beautiful garden that would be perfect."

Sondra squealed, tapping her feet, and refilled their glasses. It hadn't slipped past her that Darcie didn't cough when she took a drink anymore. Being here with her new friends and family agreed very well with Darcie. Sondra couldn't have been happier.

"Enough of the mushy, kismet stuff. I want details. Spill it, girl."

"Well, Connor couldn't believe I told you about him ripping my underwear. But he wasn't mad. He said he should give me something better to talk about."

"So, what's the something better? Don't keep me in suspense! It must be good if he's sending me gifts."

Darcie went on to tell Sondra just enough to keep her satisfied, and when she was done, Sondra sat back in her chair, fanning herself. To Sondra, the story was half the fun of sex.

"When you first came into my shop, you were a timid mouse. The second time, you were still shy, but there was a definite change, and today what I see is a blooming rose. You're still you, blushing and not giving out too many indiscreet details, party pooper, but you have definitely come out of your shell. True love, tickle fights, and steamy sex agree with you. And best of all, for me, of course, you're staying!"

"I should be overwhelmed, but I'm not. It's all so natural with Connor. I'm safe and loved. I came here in search of peace, and I found him. I found all of you," she said, wiping a happy tear from her eye before taking Sondra's hand.

"I'm selfishly happy that you're staying. I would miss my new friend."

"I would miss you, too. You're the first girlfriend I've had in years. I hid away for so long; I forgot what it was like to have friends."

"You're one of us, Darcie. We aren't letting you go anywhere."

"I have a family again!" Darcie's happy tears flowed freely.

"Yes, you do." Sondra felt a tear slip down her cheek and quickly wiped it away. She had successfully avoided crying and had no intention of turning into a puffy, snotty mess. "It's just as well that Connor didn't pay any attention to me. I'm not ticklish."

The pair burst into laughter.

CHAPTER 32

LYING on the sofa reading with her head on Connor's lap, watching TV, Darcie was thinking. She wasn't sure how he would react, but she had put it off for too long.

"There's something I need to tell you."

He turned off the television. "What's that?" He saw the worry in her eyes.

"I want to go away."

Connor's eyes grew wide with disbelief and panic. He tightened his arms around her.

It hadn't come out the way she intended. "No! I don't mean to leave Ireland or you. I mean, I want to go on a road trip by myself."

Relief washed over him. "Is that all? You had me properly worried for a minute." He took her book and placed it on the coffee table, and cuddled her into his chest. "Right, so where are you planning to visit?"

"I thought I would drive around and stop wherever I saw something interesting. It would be nice to get out on my own for a few days. Not that being with you isn't great. Well, better than great."

"I understand. But thank you for the compliment. Tell you what, I can help you plan your trip."

She didn't want to hurt his feelings. "The thing is, I don't want a plan. I came here on my own, but I did that with fear as a driving force. I'm not afraid anymore, and you have a lot to do with that. I had been scared for so long I forgot how to live. I want some time to get to know myself again."

"You want to be free."

"Well, yes. But not free from you!"

He squeezed her in his arms. "I can see why you would like some time to yourself. You've hardly had a moment's peace."

"You are my peace." Darcie laid her hand across Connor's heart, and his heart was full seeing the love in her eyes. "I want to find a little adventure. One that is mine."

Connor nodded his head. "I can accept that. You go and have your adventure, love. I won't lie and say that I won't worry about you, but as you told me before, you are a grown woman and not some bimbo without a thought in her head." He smiled. "And I will be here waiting when you get back." He watched as her eyes began to dazzle. He had reminded her of their night inside the ruins. "And what's that making a twinkle in your eyes?"

"Oh, nothing," she purred.

"Ahhh, I think I know. Good thing you're not wearing your underwear now. They would just get in my way."

Before he got too rowdy, she took his face in her hands. "This is where I belong. You are my home. You are mine, and I am yours. Those are the only reasons I need to come back and spend the rest of my life with you."

CHAPTER 33

"Will you miss me?" Darcie asked.

"I miss you every moment you're not by my side," he replied.

She let out a soft sigh as she melted into Connor's arms.

"And you promise to call me tonight after you are settled? I want to know you're safe."

"Yes, I promise."

Connor leaned into her open car window and kissed her goodbye. "Promise me you'll stay on the left side of the road."

"I have driven here, you know?"

"Not much," he grunted. "And promise me one last thing: have all the fun you can and then come home to me."

"I promise. But an O'Brian breathless kiss wouldn't hurt to remind me."

"Come here, you!"

He swung open her car door and lifted her out, crushing his mouth to hers. He held her long and tight in a kiss so deep he thought he had surely drowned them both.

She hummed into his mouth as he slowly broke away. She was draped in his arms, smiling up at him.

"Will that suffice?"

"Hmmm, I'm not sure. Maybe one more, to be certain."

He growled into her hair while she squirmed in his arms as his breath tickled her ear. "You had better get in your car while you still can. One more minute, and I'll throw you over my shoulder and haul you back to bed." He lightly pinched her bottom, making her squeal as she got back into the car.

She waved out the window as she pulled away.

"Darcie, you're on the wrong side of the road!"

She corrected herself and beeped the horn.

Connor could hear her laughing out her car window, and he whispered a little prayer. "Dear God, keep the woman I love safe and bring her home to me." He sighed and walked back inside the hotel. Flynn was there in the lobby.

"Hi, Connor."

"Hey, Flynn."

"Was that Darcie leaving? She going back to America?"

"No, she's going on a little solo tour of the island for a few days."

"I'm sure that's fine by you. Women get too clingy after a while. Am I right?" Flynn slapped Connor on the back and returned to the restaurant.

Connor went to the window, peering out at the driveway, and whispered his prayer again. "Keep her safe. Bring her home to me, please."

Darcie got to the end of the driveway and stopped. She

could turn left or right. If she was honest, she wanted to turn right back around into Connor's waiting arms. No, *you wanted an adventure, and you are going to have one!*

She turned left, heading west. *Wild Atlantic Way, here I come.*

CHAPTER 34

Darcie kept to the back roads. Mostly because she could hear Connor's voice reminding her to drive on the left. She found it difficult to do because she wanted to see everything. There was less traffic on the back roads, which meant less danger of her causing an accident, which she had already nearly done—twice. Not that she would admit any of this to Connor. A couple of days on the road by herself and her driving would be right as rain.

She continued west into County Clare and admired the beautiful homes she passed. Old cottages that could each have been a postcard, others, very modern, but they all had one thing in common: each had a beautiful garden. Many exhibited hydrangeas of various colors and some short palm trees. She couldn't figure out how palm trees could grow here, but they did, and it was lovely.

She approached an old stone church with a small grave-yard that was tucked away in a field not far from the road. It reminded her of the church Connor had taken her to see. A footpath leading to the church boasted a free-standing stone wall of large jagged rocks, all leaning against one another and stacked expertly. She thought it was incredible that it still stood. It was ancient and didn't have one bit of mortar.

The church's field was lush green with tall grass, wildflowers, and a solitary tree standing to the roofless church's left. She entered through a small iron gate that led into the graveyard. The Celtic crosses stood tall and proud, worn by time and weather, they still resonated within her. She tried to read some of the names and found a newer one that was clear.

Edith Margaret McBride 1875 - 1982 Beloved wife. Fate brought you to me, love made you stay.

Darcie couldn't take her eyes away from the epitaph. She knelt on the ground, pressed her hand to the stone, and cried. She cried for herself; she cried for her mother, her father, and she cried for the life she had left and for the one she wanted so desperately.

Darcie knelt at Edith's grave for so long that her legs went numb. With her tears dried, she walked through the open doorway of the church. Inside was empty except for a small altar with a single cross carved on it and a stone bench. She sat before the altar; her throat sore, her cheeks raw from the salty tears. She was tired of crying. This was supposed to be an adventure, not another pity party. But there was something she needed to say.

"I have asked for peace and guidance more times than I can count and never received it. I thought I was doing right. I thought I was doing good, making a difference. But I see now that all I was doing was hiding. I hid from the world; I hid from myself. No wonder you didn't answer my prayers. I wasn't sure I even believed in you anymore. I know now that I'm where I belong. Home."

The warm breeze above her whispered deeply of love. She lifted her head to the sky and breathed deep as a calm surrounded her. She had only ever felt this calm in one other place, Connor's arms.

After gathering a bouquet of wildflowers, she laid them at Edith's grave.

BACK IN HER CAR, Darcie dug around in her bag for tissues. She wiped her eyes, blew her nose, and glanced at her reflection in the rear-view mirror. Oh, dear. Puffy eyes, red nose, and red hair did not look well on her. She took a long drink from her water bottle and splashed some water on her face, dabbing it with a sock she pulled from her bag. She didn't look any better, but she felt better.

She started up the car's engine and backed out onto the street. On the road again. Within a minute, she nearly ran into an oncoming vehicle. *Left, Darcie, left!*

Not far away, she stumbled upon a charming bed-and-breakfast. It was a more contemporary house, but had an old charm. It sat on top of a hill and was painted a soft yellow, two stories with a glass sunroom and a bright blue front door. Hanging baskets of various flowers, window boxes painted the same blue as the door, and red petunias growing rampant were its crowning glory. It was lovely.

She took a chance and knocked on the door. Her cell phone battery had died, and she didn't know where the car charger had gone to; she didn't really care. A tall woman of about sixty answered the door.

"Can I help you, dear?" She sounded concerned.

"Hello, I wondered if you have a room available for tonight?"

"We have just one left. It's a room for one."

"That's perfect! I'm on my own."

The woman's eyes brightened. "Alright. I'll get my husband to help you with your bags. You come on in with me. I'm Barbara Kelly. Everyone calls me Babs." She took Darcie's hand, welcoming her.

"Darcie Hartwell. It's nice to meet you."

A man walked in from a side room. "Darcie, this is my husband, Jack."

"Hello, welcome to The Rosebud." He shook her hand.

"Get her bags and take them to the Angel Room."

"I can help you, Jack." Darcie started after him, but he waved his hand in the air, shooing her away.

"He doesn't say much. My Jack was never a man of many words, but he has a good heart. Follow me to the kitchen for a cup of tea."

Darcie looked around as they walked through the house.

"An American touring on her own, are you?"

"Yes. Well, I've been with friends. I wanted to get out by myself for a few days."

"And what have you seen so far?"

"My boyfriend," she hardly got the two words out of

her mouth without a gushing smile, "took me to the Ring of Kerry. That was stunning." Darcie sat on a stool beside the large kitchen island while Babs filled the kettle.

"Did he take you to the Kerry Cliffs?"

"Yes. The view took my breath away."

"In my opinion, they have more character than Moher." Babs placed a tray with two teacups, cream, sugar, and homemade cranberry scones in front of Darcie.

"He said the same thing. I have nothing to compare them to."

"Then you will have to go and decide for yourself. The Moher Cliffs are only a forty-minute drive from here."

"Are they? I wasn't looking at a map, so I wasn't sure exactly where I am."

"That's brave of you! Wandering Ireland with no map."

"I have a map. It's more fun this way."

"So, you happened to drive past our place?"

"That's right. I stopped at an old church not far away and ended up staying there longer than I anticipated. By the time I got back to my car, the day was nearly gone."

"My great grandmother is buried there. Edith McBride."

What were the odds of that? Darcie's eyes got wide.

"Are you alright, Darcie?"

Darcie stumbled over her words. "I saw her headstone. Her epitaph spoke to me. She must have been loved very much. I picked wildflowers and laid them on her grave."

"Ah, fate. Yes, it holds a profound meaning. She met my great grandfather while passing through town with her family. They were emigrating to America. She always said it was love at first sight. She never once regretted her decision to stay here. I don't know that I have ever known two people more in love than my great grandparents. I love my Jack, but even we don't have what they did. That was very kind of you to leave her flowers. And then you happen to come here! Fate." Babs smiled and winked.

CHAPTER 35

THE FOLLOWING MORNING, after stuffing herself with Babs' delectable breakfast, Darcie decided she wanted to be near the sea again. She got out her phone, found the charger that had been lost under the seat, got directions to the Cliffs of Moher, and away she went.

The scenery along the drive was changing. There were fewer mountains and many more massive moss-covered rocks and fairy hills. Ancient stone walls tangled with wild fuchsia, edged roads that twisted and turned like a corkscrew. She could hear Connor's voice in her head reminding her to stay on the left as she tried to concentrate on her driving and not the beautiful land.

DARCIE PUT on her purple wellies and started the hike to the edge of the cliffs. She saw a narrow dirt footpath that led higher, bordered with slim tall rocks that she used to balance herself. The path was uneven and a little wet. She had to climb over a slippery stone barrier that kept a herd of sheep grazing nearby, away from the edge and inside their pasture. As she climbed over, she laughed to herself, remembering Connor tricking her into climbing over the gate. She got over the wall and landed with a splash in an ankle-deep mud puddle. She looked down at her muddy boots, laughed.

When she reached the top, the wind had picked up. The gusts were so strong it felt like she would blow over. She waited for the wind to calm down, and when she thought it was safe, she started to walk closer to the edge. The view was spectacular. It was like standing on the edge of the world, watching the beautifully terrifying waves far below crash against the cliff face. She took a few pictures, then stood with her eyes closed, listening and taking in the breeze. If she hadn't been so enraptured by the view, she would have noticed the wind resume its assault of the over confident tourists who get too close to the edge. An over-powering gust of wind pushed her backward and felled her like a tree.

"AH, THERE'S A GOOD LASS!" a warm female voice said.

"Where am I?" Darcie asked.

"You're in the hospital. You hit your head at the cliffs. The wind picked you up off the ground! We ran a few tests, and there's no need for you to worry. Everything is fine. You need to rest, is all."

Darcie was beginning to remember and was embarrassed.

The nurse smiled at her gently. "Those winds can get violent up there. How about some tea?"

Darcie nodded her head.

"Oh, and your phone has been ringing."

Uh oh. How would she explain this? "Hi, love! I missed your voice," Connor said.

"Did you? I miss yours too." Despite her best efforts, her weak voice sent off alarm bells.

"Darcie, what's wrong? Are you hurt? Are you lost?"

The nurse came in with tea and biscuits.

"Um, well, the thing is, I kind of had an accident, but I'm fine, so you don't need to worry."

"An accident? What sort of accident?"

Darcie motioned to the nurse and asked if she would explain things to him.

"All men are worriers." She took the phone. "This is Nurse Walsh. I am here with Darcie. I assure you everything is going to be fine. She fell and hit her head, nothing serious."

"The hospital? Which one? I'm coming to get her."

"There's no need. She's much better now." Nurse Walsh quietly ducked out of the room.

"Please, Darcie, can I come get you?"

"And let you ruin my dramatic story with you riding in on a white horse? No way, O'Brian! This is one for the books. They've never had someone get knocked out from being blown over."

"Darcie! You were knocked unconscious?"

"Yep!" She said it like it was a badge of honor.

"From the wind?"

"Yep!"

So much for her safety. "Where are you?"

"I was at the Cliffs of Moher. A gust of wind blew me over, and I hit my head on a rock. The wind picked me up right off my feet!"

Connor snorted a laugh. "Well, you wanted an adventure. I suppose you're having one." She couldn't see it, but he was rubbing the sharp pain between his eyes.

"Connor, thank you."

"For what?"

"Worrying about me."

"I know when I'm beaten. But no more hospital visits! If you go again, all bets are off, and I'll drag you home kicking and screaming if I must!"

Later, Connor laughed out loud when he saw a picture of Nurse Walsh with Darcie. Her small bandage on her forehead, holding up her release papers, the pair of them giving a thumbs up.

DARCIE CONTINUED on her tour exploring The Burren. She marveled at how a place that looked as if it had been trampled by an army of giants could be beautiful. But it was. Right down to the very last flattened rock.

There were many beaches along her drive as well. Connor was certain she had stopped at each and every one. She sent him a picture of a handful of sea glass she had collected and a photo of her bare feet in the water.

He thought back on their drive through Kerry and sent a reply. "I hope that water is warm, so you aren't tempted to jump into another man's arms." His phone rang. "Hello, love. Having a good time?"

"I have something I need to tell you." She sounded serious.

"I'm listening."

"The water here is freezing. I jumped into another man's arms. We are going tonight to get married. I hope you will give us your blessing."

"Alright, you made your point, funny girl."

"You miss me?"

"You know I do. It's taking every fiber of strength I have not to run after you."

"I know. Thank you for resisting. I won't be away much longer. It's nice here. Thank you for suggesting it."

"As long as you are enjoying yourself, that is what matters to me."

"Connor, I can hear you grinding your words."

"Am not."

Silence.

"Well, suppose I am. You were knocked unconscious. I worry, is all. But I promised to respect your trip, and I will."

"Thank you."

"Just don't stay away from me too long?"

"I can't stay away from you, O'Brian. Don't you know that?"

"No," he pouted.

"Trying to guilt me into coming back? Keep it up; it's working," she said seductively.

"I miss you. I miss your smile and your blushing face."

"I thought you would say you miss me in your bed."

"I miss that too," he growled. "I'm putting you on

notice! The minute you get home, I'm hauling you to bed and will do unspeakable things with my tongue."

"Is that a promise?"

"There's my girl! Your words say one thing, but I can hear you blushing."

CONNOR FREQUENTLY CHECKED to see if Darcie had called or sent a message. He liked the silly pictures she sent. During her trip, she had gone from Dingle almost to Galway. He got worried when she sent him a photo of her car tire deep in mud, but then laughed out loud when the picture immediately following was of her full front caked in mud. All he could make out were her large green eyes. She called and told him she had gotten the car stuck, then slipped in the mud herself. The owner of the B&B had come and pulled her car out, so there was nothing to worry about.

She sent him photos of stone circles, more beaches, Poulnabrone Dolmen tomb, and ruins of whatever she could find. She even sent him a picture of a fish she caught while out boating, with the caption, "catch of the day." It was evident she was having the time of her life. But that didn't make him miss her less.

MEANDERING through the next small town, Darcie stumbled on a small art studio where she spotted a small painting of her church. The artist was watching her from his desk in the corner.

"That painting has been here for years, and no one ever paid it as much mind as you."

"I know this place."

"Do you now? Are you certain? That isn't an easy spot to find."

"It's set in a field in the mountains of Kerry. A local farmer owns the land. I've been there." she says dreamily, her expression soft. "You captured its haunting beauty so well. Is it for sale?"

"Indeed." As she walked toward him, holding the painting with the utmost care and appreciation, he told her the story she already knew. But had just a little more. "You look like her, you know?"

"Who?"

"The woman. Her name was Anne Malloy."

Darcie staggered and steadied herself on the desk.

"You could do with a sit."

He held her elbow and led her to an old armchair in his private room behind the desk. He went to make her tea, and though her sight was spinning, she made out an easel, paint supplies, and a paint-stained tarp on the floor.

"That was quite a turn you had." He said as he offered her milk and sugar. "Mind if I ask what caused it?"

She took a couple of sips of comforting tea, and as the soothing, warm liquid slid down her throat, her story bubbled up. The artist sat listening with intense interest, not once interrupting. She carefully left out her and Connor on the altar, but he seemed to have a sixth sense in his knowing eyes.

When she pulled out her necklace from under her blouse, his eyes danced, and he bustled out of the room, returning with a gold locket. Inside was a miniature portrait of Anne Malloy.

"When you say you were you but not you—this is why, you see? Christ, you could be twins!" He made the sign of the cross over his chest. "Do you know anything of your ancestors?"

She shook her head.

"And what is your name, love?"

"Darcie Anne Hartwell."

"But that isn't the name you were born with," he said in a knowing voice.

"Darcie Anne Malloy," she said, trying to take it all in. "So, her baby. It lived?"

He smiled widely and sat back in his chair with his tea, leaving her holding the locket. "Aye. She had a son, William. After Anne died, he went to the village to find his father, which was her final wish. Found him he did and told him of his mother's passing and their life. They went on from that day as father and son."

"He found his family."

"And his home. It looks like Anne wanted the same for you."

She left with the painting wrapped with great care. The artist had given it to her. A welcome home gift, he said, for the daughter of fate.

She stood looking out over the wavy hills, the distant mountains, the moss-covered fairy hills, the narrow winding roads lined with stone walls, and tree branches, all woven together. She said a prayer of gratitude. She had found what she was searching for, and now it was time to return home.

———

CONNOR WAS LISTENING to the message Darcie had left him saying she was on her way home and had a surprise for him when he passed Flynn on the sidewalk.

"Hey Connor, what's got you smiling?"

"Darcie is coming back from her road trip this evening and says she has a surprise for me."

"I had forgotten about that. Did she have fun?"

"Yes, but she's been giving me a heart attack nearly every day. She's going to be the death of me."

"All the better that she's going back to America."

Just then, Connor's phone rang. He would have to catch up with Flynn later.

CHAPTER 36

THERE WAS an unfamiliar car in Connor's driveway. Darcie assumed it belonged to one of the men from work because she didn't see Connor's car, but she could see the kitchen lights on. She went inside and stopped dead in her tracks when she saw Kristina standing beside the stove sipping tea in nothing but her underwear.

"I didn't hear anyone come in. I would have gotten dressed." Kristina feigned modesty very poorly. "Connor had to step out, but he'll be right back," she said in her venomous, sweet voice. "You look awful. I know we met, but I'm terrible with names. Who are you?"

Darcie couldn't get away fast enough. She bolted through the front door before the tears had a moment to hit her cheeks.

SHE HAPHAZARDLY PARKED at the hotel and dashed past Shamus, who started to greet her with a smile, but then saw her tears. "I hope you will be alright, lass," he called after her.

Flynn came through the lobby. "Was that Darcie I saw running through?" he asked.

"Yes. She wasn't at all herself."

"I'll have to ask Connor what's going on. See you around, Shamus."

Darcie got to her room, slammed the door, and threw her purse on the bed. She stormed out onto her balcony in a fit of tears. A knock sounded on her door. She quickly wiped her face.

"Hi, Darcie."

"Flynn, hi. What are you doing here?"

"You've been crying. You alright?" He stepped inside the doorway.

"I'm alright, I just ... " She started crying again.

Flynn stepped further inside, brought her in for a hug, and closed the door. "I'll be honest. Connor asked me to check on you. He told me everything."

"I don't understand!" she wailed.

"When Kristina left, Connor swore he would get her back. He said she was the love of his life. I think he's a fool for cheating on you. You're beautiful, smart, sexy ... " Flynn lifted her chin and kissed her.

Darcie reared back.

"Come on. He's not worth your tears. I thought you were irresistible when we met. If you had met me first, things would be different. Just give me a chance."

Panic set in. Seeing danger in Flynn's eyes, she stepped backward. He recognized her intent to flee and lunged.

"Darcie, I didn't see your car. Everything alright?" Connor called out. He stopped short when he saw Kristina sipping tea in her underwear like she owned the place.

"Nice place."

"What are you doing here?"

"Flynn asked me to stop by. For old times' sake," she said, slithering across the kitchen.

"Flynn? He knows I want nothing to do with you." He caught her hands and pushed her away when she tried to get close.

"You're no fun," she pouted. "He asked me to come into town; said you were getting in his way and wanted me to distract you." She shrugged her shoulders.

Connor didn't like the circles she was talking in and wanted a straight answer.

"It's no big deal. Flynn only wants to have a bit of fun with her. From my experience—I doubt she will turn him down."

"I don't know what you're playing at. Get your clothes on and get out."

"I'd been seeing Flynn. Behind your back, you know?" Kristina got dressed. "When she saw me, she got pretty angry. I don't know what Flynn sees in her."

Darcie. Oh God, no. Connor couldn't believe what he was hearing, but he knew Kristina wasn't lying. A shock of dread fell over him. He grabbed her arm, hauling her to his car.

"Where is Flynn right now?"

"How should I know?"

"He arranged for you to come here! You know what he's planning." Connor shook Kristina's arm in a death grip. "I'll ask one more time: where is he?"

"He's at the hotel." She rolled her eyes. "I called him when I sent her packing."

Connor pounded his fists on the steering wheel and stepped on the gas.

———

"WHERE'S THE FIRE, CONNOR?" Shamus asked.

Connor gripped Shamus' shoulder. "Did Darcie come through here?"

"Yes, a few minutes ago."

"And have you seen Flynn?"

"Now that you mention it, I saw him heading upstairs."

"Shamus, listen, Darcie's in trouble. Call the police."

Connor ran to Darcie's room and heard her screaming for help.

———

SHAMUS OPENED the door for the stretcher carrying Darcie. "May the angels be with you," he called out and wiped his eyes.

Connor got into his car and watched the ambulance leave with Darcie. He laid his head on the steering wheel and cried.

CHAPTER 37

CONNOR WATCHED HELPLESSLY as two nurses assisted Darcie into his car. She was silent as they drove away. She had refused to see him the past two days while in the hospital.

She hadn't gone down without a fight. And now she was suffering for it. Connor couldn't get her to look at him, let alone talk to him.

"The Doctor said you have broken ribs, and your shoulder needs to heal. It was dislocated. You're to have complete rest. I'm taking you home so I can take care of you. I arranged for the hotel to pack up your things."

Darcie finally spoke. "No."

"It isn't safe for you to be on your own. Please, love."

She could hear the genuine plea in his voice, and she was too weak to argue.

CONNOR HELPED Darcie to bed and brought her tea that he left on the bedside table. She turned her head away from him, closed her eyes, and fell asleep.

He, too, was exhausted. He laid down in bed beside Darcie and fell asleep. He woke up to her screaming madly for help in her sleep. She was kicking her legs, and tears were streaming down her face. Connor acted fast and gently curled against Darcie to cradle her, and she went quiet and still. He laid beside her and began to cry.

She woke up later in his arms and at first was comforted, until she remembered Kristina. She pushed him away as hard as she could and cried out in pain. He woke with a start.

"What's wrong? Do you need help?"

He got out of bed to come around and assist her. He held out his hands to help her stand, and she slapped them away.

"I don't want your help! Just leave me alone!"

He didn't understand what was going on. "Darcie, why won't you let me help you?"

She began to sob, both from the pain of trying to stand and from the pain of her broken heart.

He knelt in front of her, waiting for an answer. "This doesn't make any sense. Why won't you let me help you?"

Finally, she looked at him square in the eyes, and anger flashed across her face. He was shocked. "Because you betrayed me! You lied to me! This is your fault!"

She was crying, and he could see she was in pain. He sat back on his heels, stunned, tears stinging his eyes. Quietly he said, "I'll sleep on the sofa if that makes you happy. I don't want to upset you anymore." He stood up. "I'll bring you your medication. I can see you need it. Please try and rest now. I promise I'll not bother you."

Connor checked in on her periodically. She was sound asleep most of the time. She reluctantly had to ask him to help her to the bathroom. It was too far away for her to walk on her own. He offered to help her shower, but she refused.

THE NEXT MORNING Darcie laid in bed blankly staring out the window. The horrific events repeated over and over in her head. When Connor came in carrying a tray with breakfast, she turned her face away.

"Mum called, and she asked that you stay with them for as long as you need. You would be safe, and well looked after. I would stay here."

She said nothing.

"Darcie, please. Not for me, but yourself."

"Alright," she said in a small voice.

"Yes? Thank God." He let out a breath of relief.

She had enjoyed Sylvia and Henry, and their home was in a quiet place, and as much as she hated to admit it, she knew she couldn't take care of herself.

When they arrived, Henry and Sylvia met them at the car as Connor opened her door for her. Henry reached for Darcie, giving Connor a look of concern over his shoulder. Connor nodded in an unspoken conversation with his dad.

"Now you lean on me, lass. Take it slow. There's no rush."

Sylvia lightly touched Darcie's battered face and looked

at her through tear-filled eyes. She smiled, reassuring her that everything was going to be alright. "You're here now. No one is going to harm you. You rest and let us take care of you."

Sylvia went to the kitchen to brew tea. Connor sat at the kitchen table with his head in his hands. She laid a hand on her son's shoulder. He grasped it and cried.

"You love her?"

"Yes, I do."

"And you blame yourself for what happened to her?"

"I do because it's my fault. I didn't see. I didn't know what Flynn was."

"I didn't know you were the smartest man in the world, but right now, you are the most selfish."

"How can you call me selfish?"

"You're here blaming yourself for something you had no control over while that sweet lass in there feels God knows what. Scared, abandoned, maybe even feels like it's her fault for opening her door to a man she thought was a friend. This isn't about you. It's about her. The sooner you get over yourself, son, the sooner you can help her heal."

He let out a breath. "You're right, as usual. What can I do, mum?"

"You did right, bringing her here. You leave her with us for as long as necessary. But it would help if you got yourself sorted, son. She needs rest, and she won't get that with you hanging about."

"She doesn't want to be with me. She won't even look at me. She blames me, and so she should."

"We'll figure this out together."

"And if you don't? What if she never wants to see me again?"

"Then you will have a decision to make. To fight for Darcie or let her go. Let's not worry about that now."

THERE WAS a light knock on her door. Darcie had cried herself to sleep and blinked her eyes open. For a moment, she forgot where she was. Molly, who had snuck in and curled up beside her, woke up and licked her hand. The door opened as she tried to sit up and winced in pain. Henry peeked his head inside.

"Let me help you." He carefully got her sitting up and pulled up a chair beside her bed. "I came to sit with you if that's alright. If you want to be left alone, you say so. We don't have to talk about anything if you don't want to. I only want to sit with you." He reached over and held her limp hand.

"I would like it very much if you stayed."

"I'll sit here as long as you like."

Darcie fell back to sleep, and when she woke up, it was nearly dark. Henry was still in the chair beside her bed; he, too, had fallen asleep. But when he felt her hand move underneath his, he woke.

"There she is. Are you hungry?"

Suddenly, her stomach grumbled. "Yes, I guess I am." She managed a small smile.

"I'll bring you some dinner."

"Henry, if I could take a shower first?"

Sylvia helped her undress and get into the shower. "You just call out when you are done, and I will help you get fresh clothes on."

She hurried out of the room and burst into tears. Henry came and held her. "Oh, Henry, that poor lass. If you could see what that monster did to her. There's hardly any white skin on her."

"Shhh. She's with us now. We will take care of her and keep her safe."

"But how will we help her feel safe again? It's one thing to keep her from harm. It's another to restore her faith."

"I don't know, love. But we'll find a way."

Henry peeked in and saw her fast asleep and joined Sylvia in front of a fire with a whiskey. Suddenly, they heard her scream. They both ran to her bedroom and threw on the lights. Darcie was still asleep, but she was having a nightmare. Henry gently took her hand while Sylvia stroked her hair, speaking gentle words of comfort, the way Connor did, and Darcie quickly went quiet again without waking up. They stayed with her for a while longer before leaving her room again. They looked at each other and knew it would take a lot more than simple kindness and a hot shower to help this woman heal.

CHAPTER 38

Darcie was sitting in an oversized armchair sipping tea, staring into the empty fireplace, when Henry came in. He handed her a green velvet jewelry box. Inside was her gold necklace. Flynn had broken it. Connor had it repaired. She wiped a tear from her eye and closed the box.

"I'm going for a walk in the fields. Why don't you join me? Fresh air will do you good."

"I don't have my boots."

"Connor brought your wellies."

Standing alone beside the back door were Darcie's purple wellies. She sat on the bench while Henry helped her slide them on. She thought about the day Connor gave them to her, that most perfect day.

Henry strolled, offering his arm to Darcie for balance as he led her through the tall grass across the green field. He told her stories from his travels to pass the time and help her relax in hopes of coaxing her to talk with him.

Meanwhile, Darcie was grateful he wasn't asking any questions. Henry stopped when they could look onto the small village below. It was a lovely panoramic view of one-lane roads, a small lake, all protected by majestic mountains. A fresh breeze was carrying the scent of wildflowers and warm grass.

"It's beautiful here, Henry. Thank you for bringing me with you."

"Darcie, tell me what you see."

"I see a charming village spread out, fishing boats, small fields with sheep."

"I mean, tell me what you see in here." He laid a hand on his chest. "The land speaks to you. What is she saying right now?" he asked.

She looked around at all the colorful beauty and watched it turn gray before her eyes. "She's crying. She says that she's sorry." Just as quickly as it had all gone dark, the land before her brightened. "And that I'm loved."

"Aye. That you are." He paused a long moment. "You have nightmares. I must admit, it scared the shite out of me."

"I didn't know I had them." She was embarrassed. "I'm sorry, Henry."

"There's no need to apologize. Each time we hear you, we go in. Sylvia strokes your hair, and I hold your hand." He laid a hand over hers that held onto his arm. "You always quiet down, never waking up."

She began to cry. She was sick and tired of crying. "You do that for me?"

"We would do anything for you. When I see you and my son together, it warms this old man's heart. We consider you family. Families take care of each other. So, I'm asking if you will let us take care of you?"

"You have been taking care of me."

"I think you know what I mean. There's more to those bad dreams than what was done to you a few nights ago, isn't there?"

She nodded her head but wouldn't look him in the eye.

"Will you talk about it with me?"

She hesitated, but when she looked at Henry's kind face, she saw only love and good intentions. "Alright."

Henry helped her to the soft ground and sat beside her, patiently waiting.

"Ten years ago, my mother was diagnosed with brain cancer. She was dead in three months."

Henry thought maybe she had misspoken but let her words play out. "I am sorry for that. Losing one's mother is hard."

"Yes, it was. My dad and I were on our own to plan the funeral, deal with the lawyer ... All the things that come along with a death, you know?"

Henry nodded his head.

"It was exhausting. Dad began frequently having chest pains. He needed to rest as much as possible." She shrugged her shoulders. "So, I took on what needed to be done. I didn't mind, but it took its toll on me. I wasn't eating, couldn't sleep."

She took a long pause, focusing on the land stretched out before her, trying to summon up courage. "After the funeral, a neighbor hosted a dinner at their house. Everything had caught up with me. I needed a little quiet time, so I went into their study and closed the door." Her shoulders began to heave. "I was too weak to fight him off."

Henry sighed and wiped a tear from his eye. He was

glad the bastard was dead. Drowning was no less than he deserved.

"I left through the back door and ran home. My father found me on the bathroom floor, throwing up and crying. I told him everything. He went back and broke the man's nose. The stress caused a heart attack. I'll never forget my father collapsed on the floor, not able to move or breathe."

Henry listened as she continued. He was beginning to get a clear picture of what tormented her, and it broke his heart.

"My father was never the same. He died six years later." Darcie stared blankly at the landscape, trying to feel as little as possible and failing.

Henry put his arm around her and gave her a few quiet moments before asking more questions. "So, what is it that's causing the nightmares? The rape? The deaths?"

"It's all my fault that my dad had a heart attack. He was under so much stress with mom dying, and I was selfish. I should have stayed with him the whole day of the funeral, but I didn't. None of that would have happened if it weren't for my selfishness. He might still be here today if it weren't for me!" She couldn't hold back anymore and hung her head, sobbing. Henry brought her into his embrace while he spoke Irish to her. "Connor does that too."

"Does what?"

"Speaks Irish to me."

"Does it help?"

She raised her head. "I don't know why, but yes. I don't even know what you said, but somehow it helped."

Henry cradled her as a father would. "Darcie, you need to understand that none of that was your fault. People don't suddenly have a heart attack for no reason. They always have a condition. As for the bastard that raped you; like all predators, he waited until he saw you were most vulnerable and wouldn't be able to fight back. As long as you allow him to haunt your mind, the longer he will haunt your dreams and have control over you. You're giving him power. It's time for you to take that power back, my girl. You've a fighter in you. Fight back, Darcie. Fight for yourself."

At her wit's end, she threw her hands up. "How can you ask me to fight, Henry? It happened all over again! I'm no fighter! I'm the prey, the weak one! I should have never left the convent!" she wailed.

"Convent?"

Shocked at her hysterical slip of the tongue, she went silent.

"I only want to help you. Sylvia too, and Connor."

She stayed silent.

Seeing that he wasn't going to get another word out of her, he decided to let it rest for the moment.

———

SYLVIA MET Henry and Darcie at the door with a bright smile. "Grand day for a walk. I'm sure it did you good. I bet you're hungry."

"Yes, we are, Syl'."

Henry got Darcie settled in the armchair to rest while he and Sylvia spoke in the kitchen. Sylvia gasped and covered her mouth to keep Darcie from hearing as Henry recalled his conversation with Darcie.

"There's more she needs to tell us. So, let's get some food in her, and I promised her a whiskey. I think we'll all need one."

AFTER HAVING a casual dinner in the kitchen, they sat around a warm fire. It wasn't really cold enough for one, but it was comforting and seemed appropriate. Each had a whiskey and settled in for a long evening.

"In your time, lass. We aren't going anywhere," Henry said in a comforting voice.

"I don't know where to start. I'm sorry I lied to you. You have been nothing but kind to me."

"So far as we are concerned, you have nothing to be apologizing for," Sylvia said.

"Darcie, you said something about a convent," Henry said.

"Yes." After a long pause and a long drink from her glass, she mustered the courage to speak. "After my father's first heart attack, mom had died and, well, you know, I went to talk with the priest of our church. He knew about everything. He was concerned and wondered if I would like a place to go to rest. He suggested a convent not far away, so I could see my father whenever I wanted. I don't even know why I agreed, but I did. I was only meant to stay a few weeks. The sisters were kind to me. They didn't ask me questions, but they included me in everything. Time went by. I was suddenly enrolled to become a nun.

Looking back, I think I was looking to belong somewhere and be safe. I had never given any thought to becoming a nun before then. When I walked down the aisle, I knew it was the wrong decision. I worried about how it would affect my dad if I backed out. From that day on, I was Sister Edith Darcie. It wasn't a bad life, but it wasn't for me. Then my father died, and I decided to leave, but it took me three years to get up the courage." Darcie watched the fire flames dance for a minute before continuing. "I didn't want anything from anyone. I was dying in the convent, and no matter how much I prayed or what I did, I never felt any peace." She looked at Henry and Sylvia. "Not until I got here."

"The land spoke to you," said Henry.

Darcie smiled. "Yes, I suppose it did. I want you both to know that I had no intention of looking for a relationship. But when Connor asked me out, I couldn't say no. I know how that sounds. I'm a grown woman. I should have said no, but I didn't. I could have told him the truth, but I didn't. Once I got to know him, I didn't want to tell him the truth because I knew it would be over. I never meant to hurt him."

"You love our son," Sylvia said.

Darcie's eyes became teary again, but she knew she had to face Sylvia. "Yes."

"Why are you pushing him away?" asked Sylvia.

Darcie's voice became bitter. "Because he betrayed me. Ironic. I'm the one who lied first, but I'm the one who gets to be mad."

"What do you mean, he betrayed you?"

"He got back together with Kristina."

Sylvia gasped. Henry patted her hand and looked at a Darcie. "That tramp was lying to you, Sister."

209

Sylvia snorted. Tramp was too good a word for Kristina.

Henry went on to explain. "Flynn was jealous of you and Connor. He'd been watching you two, spying on you. He called Kristina in Dublin and hatched a plan for her to come here to tear you and Connor apart so he could have a chance with you."

Darcie's eyes got huge, and then she got angry.

"Turns out that Kristina and Flynn had been seeing each other behind Connor's back when they were engaged. So, the two of them are thick as thieves," Sylvia spat. "When Kristina told Connor that Flynn wanted you, he immediately went to find you. He handed Kristina over to the police that same evening, and she has been charged as an accomplice in your attack."

Darcie's ears started to ring, and her world went black.

———

WHEN SHE WOKE UP, she was in bed with Molly. Henry sat at her bedside, asleep. She reached for his hand, and he woke up.

"I think it would be best if I go to the hotel. I'll return to the convent as soon as I can. I've made a big enough mess here."

"You'll do no such thing!" Henry scolded. "If you think I'm going to stand by and let you dump my son and break his heart, you have got another thought coming, Sister!"

Sylvia came in the room hearing Henry's raised voice. "You're the best thing that's ever happened to him, dear. He loves you. That's why he brought you here to us. You wouldn't let him take care of you, and he wanted you safe.

He said that he wanted you to be with family. If that isn't love, then the sky isn't blue."

"But—"

"There's no buts about it. You are staying here. With your family."

Darcie was once again brought to tears. "My family. I haven't felt like part of a family in so long."

"Well, get used to it, Sister. You're one of us now," Henry declared.

"What if Connor won't forgive me?"

"If I know my son, he will. It may take him a little while to come around, but he will. He doesn't want to live without you any more than you want to live without him," Sylvia said.

Henry nodded his head in agreement.

"Would you take me to see Connor? I have some explaining to do."

Henry smiled in triumph. "I'll take you there myself tomorrow."

"Thank you." Darcie grasped his hand as he stood up and reached out for Sylvia.

"Move over, you. You've had enough time by this darling girl's bedside." She took Henry's seat and held Darcie's hand. "It's my turn. Sometimes a woman needs her mother."

Darcie slept peacefully that night. Sylvia waited for her to fall asleep before leaving the room. They never heard one whimper in the night.

CHAPTER 39

DARCIE LOOKED at herself in the mirror, disgusted with her reflection. Although no longer black and blue, her face and neck were now a hideous combination of yellow and purple. Her arms and legs were covered in the same marks. Even her hands still showed signs of her attack.

Sylvia helped Darcie dress, choosing a white, loose-fitting, long-sleeved cotton shirt that buttoned up the front and soft black leggings. Sondra had sent over a gift basket of soft clothes and other comforting presents. Darcie was very grateful at the moment for Sondra's ability to foresee the need for such clothing. She looked like she was ready for bed, not for begging forgiveness. But Darcie wanted to cover up as much as possible. She wasn't looking for pity.

They drove in silence to Connor's. Darcie was thinking of what she would say. Henry didn't want to interrupt her thought, so he turned on the radio low for some background noise. He turned it to an oldies station. She knew he had chosen the station deliberately, but it lightened her mood, so she was grateful.

"Henry, can we go to the hotel first? I need something from the safe in my room."

———

"MUM? I WASN'T EXPECTING YOU."

Sylvia walked into Connor's office and closed the door. "We need to talk."

Sylvia sat down for a serious talk with her son. Connor's eyes filled with tears as he listened to Sylvia recount Darcie's story.

" ... It was at her own mother's funeral, too, adding insult to injury. Her father had a heart attack defending her honor that day, and she blames herself for his death. Your father and I believe this is the root of her nightmares."

Connor's head began pounding.

"Darcie was told nothing of the plot between Flynn and Kristina, and she believed you and Kristina had gotten back together."

"That's why she wouldn't so much as look at me? Oh, mum, I've made a real mess of things." He rubbed the stabbing pain between his eyes.

"Don't be too hard on yourself, son. She didn't tell you, and you had no way of knowing what Flynn said or what the police didn't tell her. But there's more. It's not my story to tell, so that I won't be sharing. But your father is driving her up to see you right now. All I ask is that you hear her out and after she is finished, ask yourself one question: Can you have a moment of peace while Darcie walks through life without you? You told me you love her. That is about to be tested. For both your sakes, I hope you make the right decision. That's all I'm going to say on the matter."

Connor knew his mother well enough to know not to push her, so with a simple goodbye, he allowed her to leave.

CONNOR WAS WAITING for Darcie outside his front door. He fought the urge to carry her out of the car, bring her inside, and lock the door.

She sat in the car staring at him through the windshield and could feel his stare burning into her skin.

Henry got out and opened her car door for her and helped her to stand. She felt wobbly all of a sudden and nearly fell over. Henry caught her in his arms and gestured to Connor. Connor eased his arm around her waist and offering his arm as a crutch. He smiled lightly at her.

"Thank you." She turned her head to look back at Henry for confidence.

"I'll come back around for you, lass," he called and gave her a thumbs up.

Connor slowly walked her inside. "Would you like to sit on the sofa?"

"That would be nice."

"Can I get you something? Tea? A chocolate biscuit? That neighbor girl was here the other day."

She couldn't help but crack a laugh. "Tea, thank you."

Connor laid a tray with tea and chocolate biscuits on the coffee table.

"I thought that was all a joke," she said.

He smiled weakly. "No, the little shite sells me biscuits every chance she gets."

"How bad could they be?" Darcie took a bite. The look on her face said it all. Connor had a napkin ready so she could spit it out.

They sat in silence for a minute, measuring up each other. Connor fought the urge to cry. He didn't care what she had to tell him. Nothing could hurt him worse than being without her. And her face! The horrific event still stained her beautiful, sweet face. Anger burned his throat. To keep himself calm, he started the conversation.

"Mum explained to me that you didn't know about Flynn and Kristina."

Darcie nodded.

"I'm sorry. It never occurred to me you didn't know. I assumed the police told you."

"No, they didn't."

"If I'd told you myself, none of this would have happened. The truth is, I couldn't bring myself to talk about it. I could have had you here with me this whole time instead of sending you to my parents."

"They said you wanted me to be safe and with family."

"Aye. Can you forgive me?"

"Forgive you? For what?"

"I'm supposed to keep you safe. I failed. I didn't know what Flynn was. If—"

"Please don't. None of this is your fault. I blamed you, and I couldn't be sorrier. I should have known you wouldn't betray me. You saved me." Her lip trembled. "What if you hadn't—"

"Shhh, let's not think of that now."

"I'm the one asking for your forgiveness. Connor, I love you."

The tears Connor fought began to drop. Darcie took his hands. There was an awkward silence.

"There's more I need to tell you. All I ask is that you listen, and then I will accept whatever decision you make."

"If it's about the bastard that raped you, mum gave me the short version of that story."

"Oh. Yes."

"Why didn't you tell me?"

"It's not such an easy thing to say. But I will tell you now if you want me to."

"No, no need to drag this out any longer. You have bad news for me, and I think I know what it is. My love, we—" Connor stopped short when he felt a wedding ring on her finger. He sat in silence, stunned. He ran his finger over the gold band over and over as if he could erase it. His head started to throb. "You're married?" Outraged, he yelled, "All this was a game to you? I fell in love with you, Darcie! You said you wanted to have a life with me!"

The look of betrayal he flashed was too much for her to bear. She looked away in shame. He stood up and paced the room.

"Please let me explain," she pleaded.

"Explain what? That you're a bored housewife whose husband doesn't understand her, so she thought she would find herself a good Irish fuck? And I was stupid enough to fall for your lies!"

He was yelling at her. She knew she deserved it, but she needed him to hear her. So, she yelled right back.

"This isn't a wedding ring, you idiot!" Darcie had never

once raised her voice or insulted him. Right now, at this moment, she meant business. Having got his attention, she dropped her voice back to normal. "Not the kind you think it is, anyway."

"Sure, and I'm that stupid to fall for this! What other kind of wedding ring is there, Darcie?"

"I'm a nun!"

He couldn't believe what she just said. A nun? He was about to call her out as a liar when she held out the ring for him. He took it and read the inscription on the inside "Sister Edith Darcie 6/3/2016."

This was all too much. Darcie didn't even believe in God, for Christ's sake! Now she says she's a nun! Connor dropped the ring on the floor and stormed out the back door, slamming it behind him.

Darcie curled into herself, crying until she had wept herself to sleep.

CONNOR STOMPED OUTSIDE IN A RAGE. A nun! What sort of nun goes around acting as she has? He had to keep moving, so he walked.

She blames me for her attack, refuses to speak to me, and then shows up begging forgiveness for lying about her whole life? That's some nerve!

He ended up by the cliffs, and as he stood looking across the sea, he saw Darcie's face, he heard her laugh. He remembered their first kiss. Nothing had shaken him like that before. He remembered his need for her and how all he wanted from the moment he laid eyes on her was to make her happy. He pictured her dancing in the parking lot. The woman he had dinner with that blushed with any compliment.

He walked down the cliff path and remembered what it felt like when she slipped. He thought she was a goner, and it nearly killed him. He continued along the beach and spotted a piece of sea glass. It made him think of her birthday and all they had shared that night. That wasn't a lie. The afternoon in the pagan church. She said she loved him that day, and that was the day she had allowed him to break through her defenses. That wasn't a lie. Maybe the rest wasn't either. "Will you ever have a moment's peace while she walks this earth without you?" That is what his mother had asked.

He turned back to the house.

DARCIE WAS asleep on the sofa, curled up tight as if protecting herself. She had always slept comfortably in his house. But not today. He looked at her innocent face, stained with bruises and tears. His anger melted away. He rested his lips on her forehead.

"Connor. I thought you left. I thought you hated me," she cried. "I called you an idiot. I'm so sorry."

"Shhh, acushla. I'm here now. I'm sorry I left. I shouldn't have yelled at you, and I'm sorry for all the things I said." He wiped her tears while whispering Irish words to soothe her. "Can I hold you?" he asked.

"I'd like that." He held her gently as she breathed in

deep and leaned back, relaxing into his chest. "I've missed you. I've missed this. Being close to you," she said.

"I missed you too." He took a minute to enjoy having her back in his arms. "I knew there were things about your life you were holding back from me, the truth is, I didn't always want to hear what those things were. I didn't always give you a chance to explain. I thought that if you didn't speak the truth about whatever was back in America, then it didn't exist."

"Sometimes, it feels like the past ten years didn't really exist. I wasn't myself. The day I left the convent, Mother Mary Francis told me that I could either dominate or hide in this life and that I needed to choose. I chose to run. I didn't know what I was running to, but I knew that I couldn't stay at the convent anymore. The nuns offered me a safe place, and at the time, I needed it. But eventually, I realized I was hiding. I didn't want to hide anymore."

CHAPTER 40

DARCIE TOLD HIM EVERYTHING, leaving nothing out. Connor patiently listened. Then she came to the end of her story.

" ... and then I saw you. Everything changed. It was like I had been living in black and white, and the moment I saw you, everything turned to color. Does that sound absurd?"

"No, I felt the same way when I saw you in the parking lot."

"The parking lot?" she asked.

"I was in the hallway, the one where we first met, looking out the window when I saw a woman dancing and laughing. She looked like someone who didn't have a care in the world. It was a moment of pure joy I witnessed. I wanted to know how one could be so happy and free. I fell in love with you that moment. Then you appeared in my hallway. The woman of my dreams. I was a goner." He stroked her hair. He realized then the gesture was now as much for him as it was for her. "Only an Irish nun would have the courage to leave everything behind to come find her true love."

"Is that what I was doing?"

"We need each other, Darcie Hartwell. Don't try and deny it now."

"I won't. I do need you. I need all of you. You're my family, my home. Connor, can you ever forgive me?"

"I forgave you the moment I slammed the door. I knew it was a mistake. Can you forgive me for leaving like that?"

"Of course." Her head fell back into his chest with a sigh of relief.

"Would it be alright if I kissed you?"

"I wish you would."

"You are mine, Darcie Hartwell, I am yours and nothing, and no one is going to harm you or come between us again."

Henry sneaked through the front door, quiet as a mouse. He wasn't one for eavesdropping, but he needed to know if Sister had brought his son around. If she hadn't, then he just might, for Connor's own good, of course, knock his block off. Standing motionless, Henry listened. He overheard Sister refer to himself and Sylvia as her family, and Connor profess his undying love. He couldn't decide if he wanted to cheer or cry.

He left her suitcase beside the door, smiled and let himself out.

CONNOR AND DARCIE fell asleep on the sofa. He woke

up to Darcie nuzzling her head into his chest. "Hello," he said softly and stroked her hair.

"Can I stay?"

His heart burst. "Yes. Stay. Stay forever."

She let out a sigh, laid her hand across his heart, and murmured, "Home."

They stayed on the sofa awhile longer, enjoying each other's company, when Darcie's stomach growled. Connor looked out the window. It was nearly dark.

"You must be starving."

"I think it's your mother's cooking. I've never eaten so much in my life, and now I'm probably used to it."

"I knew she would take good care of you. Well, I can't cook like mum, but I might have your favorite chocolate cake in the kitchen." Her eyes got hungry. "How about we get fish and chips and then have dessert?"

"Sounds perfect."

WHILE EATING THEIR DINNER, Connor asked a question. "There is one thing I don't understand."

She got worried. "What's that?"

"I thought nuns aren't allowed to have possessions, money, and such. How did you make it here?"

She was surprised she'd forgotten about that. "My father left everything to me. I was prepared to give it all to the church, but Mother Mary Francis advised me to put everything into the bank. She said I might need it someday, but she would accept my donation if I didn't. I think she knew I wasn't cut out to be a nun before I realized it myself.

So, no mention of it was made to the church, and nobody asked questions.

I assume she had something to do with that. She was the one person, other than my father, who tried her best to look out for me. She may not have been a girlfriend to me, but she was my guardian angel. I owe her a lot. That is my one regret, leaving her. I miss her." She sighed. "I'm quite the catch, you know? My father was a wise investor and left me well off. I sometimes wonder if he knew I would eventually leave the convent."

"Aaah, so I found myself an heiress, did I? You can pay for dinner next time."

CHAPTER 41

THE NEXT MORNING, Connor woke up with Darcie in his arms. She hadn't cried in the night, and Connor had the first full night's sleep since she had left him.

"Could I take a shower?" she asked.

"You don't need my permission. This is your home."

"I might not need your permission, but I do need your help."

"Of course, I'll help you. Anything you need." He had to choke back the lump in his throat.

When they had gone to bed, she had insisted on changing into her pajamas in the bathroom. He assumed her modesty had settled in while they were apart. Now, in the morning light, she sat on the bed and allowed him to undress her. It was the first time he'd seen her naked since the attack. Connor fell to his knees, sobbing.

Darcie stroked his hair. "I know. It looks bad, but I'm getting better."

"I can't help but look at you like this and think what would have happened if I hadn't found you in time."

"But you did find me. You saved me. Flynn tried to break me, break us, but he failed." She raised his head to look at her face. "If you give him any more of your thoughts, then he holds power over us. Don't give him that power."

"There's something new I see in your eyes." He studied her. "Fortitude."

"Your dad helped me with that. He was the one who told me about not giving power to my fears. As much as you wanted me here with you, you did the right thing by having me go." She hugged him. "Thank you."

Dear God, he had missed her. He forgot himself for a minute. Her touch was too much for words.

She took his face in her hands and held him close. She hadn't noticed the dark circles under his eyes, and his cheeks looked thin. "I'm sorry I shut you out. I don't want to live in the past. I can't go back to black and white. I had to let it go, but I couldn't. Not without you."

"My love, you're amazing." He held her another minute and felt her skin get cold. "I think it's time to relight your affair with the shower."

She laughed as he turned on all the water heads at once. She held her arms out with her head basking as the water rained down.

He took great care in sponging her body and then washed her hair. He was pampering her, and she was lapping it up. She moaned lazily with her eyes closed.

"You better cool it, O'Brian. If I had known you would do this, I wouldn't have bothered with the spa."

"You're home now. Get used to it."

CHAPTER 42

CONNOR WAS a bag full of nerves. When he arrived at the convent gates, he sat in the car looking at what used to be Darcie's home. Darcie had made herself a prison from what was meant to be a sanctuary.

As he stared at the large red brick house, he pictured her running down the sidewalk to the gates the day she left. She was scared, but determined. He was feeling a bit like that, too.

It's now or never. He walked up to the gates and rang the bell. A nun appeared by the side of the house and made her way down the sidewalk. She was an older woman with a kind face.

"May I help you?" she asked.

"Please, I'd like to see Mother Mary Francis. My name is Connor O'Brian. I think she'll know who I am."

"I am Mary Francis. I know who you are, Mr. O'Brian. Come in."

She led him quietly to the house. Her silence made him more nervous. She led him through the kitchen, made tea for them both, and walked down the hall to her office. After they were seated at either side of her desk, she spoke.

"You have come a long way to see me. I assume this is not for a casual social visit?"

Darcie had described her as someone who didn't mince words. She wasn't kidding. "No, it isn't." He took a sip of his tea. "I've come to speak with you about Darcie. There's no easy way to say this, so I'll just get on with it. Someone tried to rape her a few weeks ago."

Francis gasped and covered her mouth.

"He failed. But he beat her severely."

"How did she escape?"

"I found her. I nearly killed him."

She saw guilt in his eyes. "You saved her. Why do you blame yourself for the actions of a monster?"

"I thought he was a friend of mine. I couldn't have been more wrong."

"Mr. O'Brian, we are not responsible for the actions of anyone but ourselves. If you had not found Darcie, then she would be far worse off. Take comfort in that."

"Yes. That's what my parents said, too."

"When she came to us, she was a broken woman. She hardly spoke a word for months. A priest was counseling her, but it was a long road. She asked to be more involved with the charity work. I thought it would be good for her, so I agreed. Slowly, I saw her become human again. When she wanted to take the veil, I was hesitant, but allowed her to begin the journey. In truth, when she took her vows, I was uneasy. I did not think it was the right choice. But I also knew she could not make a life outside our walls. She was not strong enough. We could give her the best chance."

She paused and sipped her tea. Her expression was one of deep regret. "It was not long after her vows that I saw her unhappiness. Then her father had another heart attack, and she retreated into herself. Two years later, he died. He was the only human being left in this world that Darcie truly loved." She looked Connor straight in the eyes. "People think faith saves you in a time of crisis. But for some, all the faith in the world will not restore peace."

She paused again and nodded. "Mr. O'Brian, while I cannot condone her running away, I can understand her motive. Her peace was stolen, and no matter how hard she tried, she could not get it back. I would often hear her screaming at night in her sleep. It broke my heart to see such a sweet woman be brought to nothing but a mere shell of herself. I did what I could, but it was not enough. She needed someone else. She needed you." She watched as a tear ran down his cheek. "Darcie told me about you. I heard joy in her voice. I got worried when she had not called in for over a week, so I called her. When she answered, I was speaking to the broken woman once again. I assumed you had broken her heart. She would not give me an explanation. When she called again, I heard her joy restored, and I heard your voice in the background."

He laid his teacup on the desk and wiped his tears. He felt as though he needed to make his plea to a judge. "I only want to protect her, love her, and make her happy. That's all I've wanted since the moment I saw her."

"I see your sincerity. My question for you is: what are you doing here?"

It was time for his closing argument. "You said Darcie's father was the last soul on the earth she loved. Well, you're mistaken. She loves you. You gave her comfort, safety, and friendship when she needed it most. She ran from this way of life, but she didn't run from you. She misses you. So, being that you are the closest thing to a parent she's had these past years, I've come to ask your permission to propose to her."

Francis stared at him with a blank face for a minute. He shifted in his seat. Then he saw a tear fall down her cheek, and she smiled.

"I was hoping that was the purpose of your visit. Yes, you have my permission, and you have my blessing."

"Sure, you've a way of making a man sweat, Sister! I can't live without her. I thought you were going to refuse me, and I would have to burn in hell for eternity for going against a nun's wishes!"

As FRANCIS WALKED with Connor to his car, she held onto his arm. "You are just what she needs. You found her when she could not even find herself and brought her back to life. Call it God or fate, it is all the same, but you were destined for her. I do not doubt that." She patted his arm. That was as close to a hug as he could expect. "Now, go home and make our girl the happiest being on earth."

She may not have wanted to hug him, but he wasn't leaving without a sign of affection, so he kissed her cheek, making her blush. "Thank you!" he said.

"I will expect a wedding invitation."

"You'll be first on the list, I promise!"

CONNOR PULLED up to the footpath leading to the pagan church. Darcie looked at him, blushing at the memory of what they had done there. He looked at her and laughed.

"I've a surprise for you."

"If it's anything like last time ... "

He flashed her his devilish smile. As they walked hand in hand down the path, a breeze swirled around them. She took in a deep breath and closed her eyes. She heard the faint voice of Anne Malloy.

"What do you hear?"

"Whispers of love."

He smiled and led her on. When they approached the church, he stopped.

"We aren't going inside?"

"You can go inside now whenever you like as often as you wish."

"I don't understand."

"This is yours now."

"What do you mean?"

"I spoke with the farmer who owns this land. I made him an offer, and he was that glad to sell it to me."

She looked around her at the fields, the mountains, and the running stream. "Connor, I don't know what to say."

"Say thank you."

"Thank you." She pressed her hand to his cheek.

"You can sit there by the stream and read or whatever you like. I can build you a rotunda there if you want and a new roof on the church. But this is now yours. A haven, a sanctuary, a place to pray, weep, laugh, or scream." He winked.

She walked to the door, and this time she did not feel the sadness. She stepped inside and ran her hand along the stone altar, looking around at the walls. She saw it for what it was: hers.

She stepped outside and turned around. "A red climbing rose bush would be nice on this wall. Don't you think?"

"I have another gift for you." He knelt and held out a small purple satin box. Inside was a ring of gold with a round sparkling emerald surrounded by a starburst of diamonds. "Darcie Hartwell, I want to change your name for the last time."

She took his hands and lifted him off his knee. "Yes! A thousand times, yes!"

He threw his arms around her and twirled her around with a whoop.

Connor stood behind her with his arms wrapped around her shoulders as they looked out over the land.

"Connor, you've given me so much. I don't know if I'll ever be able to thank you enough. But I think I have a good way to start." She took his hands and slid them down to her abdomen, and held them there.

He didn't understand the gesture until he looked into her eyes. "Darcie? You're—but you can't be. I mean, you said you couldn't."

"I guess fate had other plans."

He turned her toward him and knelt, placing his hands on her abdomen with a light caress. He looked up at her.

Tears filled his eyes. "Are you sure? I mean, you were beaten so badly."

"Yes. I knew about the baby, and they monitored us. I went back to the doctor yesterday. I heard the heartbeat. I wanted to hear it before I told you. Just to make sure it was all real."

He continued to cry. "When?"

"I found out when I hit my head. When the doctor told me that I didn't need to worry about the baby, I thought he must have talked to the wrong woman. He assured me there was no mistake. I wanted to come right home and tell you. But I needed a couple of days for myself first."

Connor nodded his head.

"I didn't need a doctor to tell me when. It was conceived right here. The place where you found me. The place where I surrendered everything to you." She smiled at him and held his face in her hands.

"Thank you." He lifted her shirt a little and kissed her. He held onto her waist and said, "She's going to be the light of our lives."

"She?"

He kissed her stomach again. "I love you. I love both of you."

He stood, and she wrapped herself in his arms. "We love you too."

He rocked her in his arms.

"Connor?"

"Yes?"

"I'd like to get married in our secret garden."

"That's a relief. I already started readying it."

She looked at him, laughing. "So, this place is all mine?"

"Aye, it is."

"And just how far away would the nearest person be right now?"

He smiled. "Oooh, they surely would be way over on the next mountain, I should say."

"Hey, Connor?"

"Yes?"

"I'm wearing red underwear."

EPILOGUE

"DARCIE, WE GOT A POSTCARD FROM SONDRA," Connor called out as he walked inside the front door.

Just arriving home, he brought in the mail. He shook his head, sighing out a laugh. He still couldn't walk through the secret garden without being plagued by the memory of Sondra smiling at him and waving hello with her foot, not missing a beat when he stumbled upon her and his cousin Simon at it behind the hydrangea bushes. She really was incorrigible.

He had quickly walked away only to discover Shamus and Nan kissing underneath the archway of climbing roses! But he couldn't help but laugh. The two pairs had been inseparable from each other since his and Darcie's wedding.

"IT'S DONE, Boss. Both of them."

"Good."

"What next? You want me to get her?"

"No. Not yet. Keep an eye on her. A close eye."

GET A FREE BONUS
CHAPTER OF ESCAPE

Want a free bonus chapter?
Get your free bonus chapter here

BREAK FREE
THE O'BRIANS, BOOK TWO

Sometimes true love is shadowed by lust ...

"You had it coming! You hear me? This is all your fault!" The heavy crash of an upturned table echoed throughout the house from the kitchen.

"Shhh, be very quiet," she whispered. She crawled into the dark closet to the furthest corner. "He won't come in here." She felt around for her flashlight and then found the glass stuck in her arm. She winced in pain as she carefully removed the shard with her trembling fingers. "I'll be alright. Don't worry." She wrapped her bleeding arm in her dress and waited, listening for a sign that it was all over.

Love hurt. He always apologized, but his remorse was always short-lived. It all came down to the twisted sacrifices made within the confines of marriage. Thanks to him, she had learned that nobody would ever love her. Nobody was going to keep her safe. And thanks to him, nobody would be given the opportunity again. She had to depend on herself.

Sondra Keane's eyelids flew open. Her panicked gaze darted around the room. To the left was her illuminated Waterford crystal lamp, to the right a painting of the Youghal harbor. Straight ahead was her open bedroom door. She exhaled sharply and dropped her head into her soft pillow. She was home; she was safe. As her heartbeat slowed, she brought the bedcovers up to her chin and tucked herself into a cocoon.

All this time and he still managed to prey upon her sleep. Frightful dreams of memories long gone. Memories she would love nothing more than to erase and had tried, time and time again, but to no avail.

But there was no time to dwell on that. Distressing as the memories were, she refused to allow her morning to be spoiled. After allowing herself a brief nap, the rising sun peeked through her blue silk curtains and pushed her eyelids back open.

Sondra stretched her long limbs with a wide yawn as she squinted in the morning sunlight. She wasn't a natural morning person, but she was determined to beat the clock. It took a few minutes, but she resolved to crawl out from under her smooth-as-cream silk bedsheets. One consolation to dragging herself out of bed was the corner bakery. It was Friday. That meant they would have her favorite pastry and open in precisely—she picked up her bedside clock to check —twenty-three minutes. That was something worth getting out of bed for.

But then again, she would leap out of bed with an Olympic dismount if it meant the anxious feeling clawing under her skin would take a flying leap out the nearest window. Lately, her terrible memories were constantly bubbling up in her dreams, but it wasn't only that. There was something... else. She couldn't describe it, this hunch.

She splashed her face with water and patted it dry with a soft towel. She was naturally beautiful and knew it, but didn't take it for granted and spent little time looking over her reflection. No sense in worrying over what nature had in store for her. She would take it in stride—with the exception of her face cream. I mean, really, she couldn't be expected to do nothing while her smooth, milky skin gradually sagged and discolored. As she rubbed a few drops of cream on her face, she thought of what needed to be done that day. It was a big weekend, and there was a laundry list of things to do. On her mirror was a post-it note she had placed there the night before: *Mail Mrs. Donaghue's order.*

That made her think of the irritating postman. She always tried to avoid him. Perhaps this vexing premonition could go and haunt him instead? She cackled to herself as she brushed her golden hair into a ponytail. All she knew was she didn't care for it, whatever it was. No, it didn't suit her. Not in the least.

She opened her front door, hip-checked the feeling to the side, and eagerly skipped off to the bakery.

Why the wicked old witch Donaghue thought she needed French lace lingerie, Sondra didn't know and, quite frankly, didn't care. The woman spent more money in her shop than any other customer. So, if she wanted hot pink lingerie, Sondra would make sure she got it. However, she felt sorry for whomever had to see her in it. The woman desperately needed a razor, not to mention an attitude adjustment.

Unlike her friend Darcie, who was getting married the

next day. Darcie was everything good in the world: kind, innocent, and sweet as pie with her blushing cheeks and beautiful expression. They had been instant friends when she walked through the door of Sondra's boutique. Shy, gentle, and lonely, she was. Those days were gone. Since then, Darcie had met the love of her life and made friends who she treated like family.

Sondra considered herself blessed to be included in that circle. Although she was generous, kind, and outgoing, and had excellent taste in fashion, women didn't like her. They didn't bother to look past what they were envious of to see what was in her heart. She was everything they wanted to be: naturally thin and beautiful, and that was all that mattered to the shallow women who shunned her. She was good enough to buy clothes from, but that was all. Nothing more, nothing less. Sondra would never admit it out loud, but she'd had a somewhat isolated life before Darcie arrived. Sure, she had her men, many dates, but no real friends and no family. In Darcie, she had both.

Steam my bridesmaid gown, close the shop early, pick up pizza, ice cream, crisps, pickles, chocolates; too bad Darcie's pregnant. I could go for a nice whiskey... Everything else for the weekend was already packed and sitting beside the front door.

All of that important business would be attended to later, and it would require her full attention. But she had another bit of business to attend to right now, and no morning was complete without him.

Brayden spotted Sondra coming up the sidewalk as he placed loaves of fresh bread in his window. She was the sort of woman every man noticed. He paused a moment to admire her. Other than his wife, she was the most beautiful woman he knew. There had been a time when he had wanted to marry her, but she wasn't the marrying kind. Or so that's what she had told him. But he knew better.

Sondra was skilled at appearing like she had everything figured out. She was kind, helpful to those in need, smart as a whip, and fun to know. Everything about her was beautiful—apart from the foul temper. The woman could rip the hind leg off a horse. He laughed to himself. The fact was that even that part of her was beautiful. She didn't showcase her temper, but Lord help you if you got her Irish up.

But she was lonely. However, nobody would ever hear her admit it. Brayden often wondered if the day would ever come when someone would break through the barrier she'd built so high and sweep her off her feet. If ever there was a woman who needed it, it was Sondra. Although many tried, all had failed. But there had to be someone who could break her free.

"You're looking well this fine morning, Keane."

"Thank you. Yourself as well." Sondra beamed her smile at the bakery owner as she swept through the door. They were old friends and had dated for a short while. He was the nicest man she knew, not to mention a hell of a lover. But he wasn't for her. She much preferred a man who was a little rough around the edges. Someone who kept her guessing, on her toes, and most importantly, who didn't ask questions and didn't stay. Brayden's wife and four children were not the life she had ever wanted. "How is Maria?"

He grinned. "She's grand."

"I know that smile. You've not gone and knocked her up again?"

"Maybe. She has an appointment today with the doctor." He beamed with male pride. "Is it a coffee or a tea morning?"

"Coffee."

Domestic bliss was the only term that came to mind when she thought of Brayden and Maria. It made Sondra want to run away screaming. Brayden knew it and handed her a large coffee with extra sugar and cream and three chocolate cherry danish pastries. The only three in the bakery. Usually, he only made her two, but knowing that talk of marital bliss made her queasy, he thought today would be perfect for an extra treat.

Sondra held the paper bag open and took a deep breath of the fresh-baked heavenly confections. Her ravenous eyes nearly teared up with appreciation.

Brayden chuckled. "How you can eat that I'll never understand." He'd created the recipe special to tame her wild sweet tooth.

"Just keep baking them for me, and don't ask questions."

"How about a bagel with egg, spinach—"

"Stop right there."

"Alright. Have it your own way then." Brayden shook his head with a grin. "All set for the wedding?"

"Of course! It's going to be perfect if I have anything to say about it—and I do."

"Darcie is lucky to have you."

"I'm the lucky one. Lots to do today, so I've got to run." Sondra turned to leave and paused at the door, holding it open for an elderly couple. "Tell Maria to come and see me. I'll make her the best-dressed mother-to-be in town. She will have gotten rid of her maternity clothes."

It had been three years since their last child. They had said that was their last. Apparently not. Sondra smirked, thanked Brayden, and headed on her way, eager to sink her teeth into her morning goodies.

Sondra began her usual morning stroll inside serene Killarney Park to her usual spot where she could savor the morning air and her danish. She walked along the weathered path to a bench surrounded by low-hanging trees, ferns, and boulders so old that when a breeze circled, they sang melodies of the ancestors and battles long since gone but not forgotten.

Soon the leaves would change on the trees. Many shades of green that made up the forest would turn into amber, red, and brown. That was her favorite time of year. For now, however, the cheerful wildflowers that dabbled the forested landscape were all the color she needed.

While she sat, she admired the view around her and savored the subtle sounds of the forest on this fine, soft morning. The night's rain had left a thin veil of low-lying mist across the lush ground. She watched as the sunlight filtered through the trees and burned away the fog. The dew dropped wildflowers shimmered and perked up their faces to bask in the light while bees and butterflies drifted from petal to petal.

It was all peaceful and quiet until a couple jogged past. Americans dressed in skintight, tasteless, neon matching outfits right down to their fluorescent orange trainers. They shouted between their puffs, saying how envious they were of places such as this one. She wondered how they could truly appreciate such a place when all they were doing was running and disturbing the tranquility. Thankfully, they did not stop, and their din quickly departed with them. Sondra shook her head at the back of them and continued.

Lustrous sunlight filtered through the trees, a faint breeze carrying the scent of wildflowers, and the lazily moving stream that led to the lake were scenes that could only be truly appreciated by stopping and paying them the admiration they deserved. Unfortunately, those two obnoxiously dressed joggers didn't know what they were missing. More's the pity. To Sondra, it was simply home. Sometimes she forgot what a privilege it was to call a place as beautiful as Ireland home. Ridiculous as the couple was, she was grateful to them for the reminder. Sondra enjoyed the scenery and smiled to herself, thinking of Darcie. She always said there was some kind of magic here on their fair island. Maybe she was right?

Sondra took one large, slow bite into her favorite danish and licked the chocolate from her fingers with a pleasured smile. Brayden had made these with extra chocolate. God bless him. As the rich chocolate mixed with the sweet cherry on her tongue, her eyes rolled back in her head. That was one thing no other man could ever do.

Sondra stared aimlessly ahead. Some would call it debauchery; she didn't care. She just called it living on her terms. She wasn't one for asking permission or waiting on someone else to make things happen. Nobody would take care of her better than she took care of herself. But it had been too long since she had been in a man's arms. Although she preferred waking up alone, she couldn't shake off the ache for the touch of a rough pair of hands. And although caution wasn't a word in her vocabulary, Sondra backed off men after Darcie was attacked a couple of months before. She wouldn't say that she was afraid, but a little more prudence couldn't hurt. Not that it mattered. She had met no one worth taking her lipstick off for, never mind anything else.

But if she didn't find a bit of male company soon, she would be very cranky and may do something drastic. Wasn't it only a couple of nights ago when she had practically scratched a hole in the sofa watching the evening news? The newscaster was short, bald, and baby-faced, but he had a deep voice incongruous with his looks that drove her wild.

Sondra's restlessness was waking up. There was only one way to deal with it. She gnawed at her lip. A night of good sex would do the trick. But, at this point, she would settle for a pinch on her bum. For Sondra, sex was as easy as breathing; it was the other stuff that came with it she found troublesome. Words like commitment, love, trust, and faith: all the words that define marriage and relationships. Those made her want to head for the hills as fast as her feet would carry her. As much as she was looking forward to Darcie's wedding, she knew that would never be a path she took for herself.

Her bundle from Brayden was now empty, and she had devoured every last delectable crumb. She took a deep breath and one last appreciative look around her and headed home. Now that she was adequately fortified, she was ready to take on the day.

"Good day to you, Mr. O'Dwyer." Sondra's elderly neighbor was walking his dog.

"Good morning, Sondra." He smiled, watching her play with his small dog, appropriately named Bitsy. "You're looking well this fine morning." He admired her golden hair in the morning sunlight. She was the most beautiful woman he'd ever seen, apart from his late wife, of course, a true natural beauty.

"As are you." She took notice of his clothes and that he was using his cane for support more than usual. "You're looking very distinguished in your suit."

"I should hope so. You gave me this suit."

Sondra straightened his lapel and noticed that the jacket looked slightly loose around his shoulders.

He enjoyed her fussing over him. "Ah, Sondra, love, you make our island beautiful with the clothes you sell and even more beautiful just by waking up in the morning."

She smiled sweetly and laid her hand on his cheek. Nobody gave compliments as charming as his. "Have a date for breakfast, do you?"

"No, no. Nothing like that. But if you say yes, I would."

She grinned at him as she waited for his answer.

"I've a doctor's appointment. I figure if I look handsome enough, perhaps I can charm a nurse to run away with me. Unless you finally saw sense and have decided to take me for yourself?"

"You know I like things as they are." She knelt to pet the small dog. "But if I ever feel the urge to marry, you will be the first one I call." She stood up with Bitsy in her arms. "Speaking of marriage, I have to be going now. My friend is getting married tomorrow, and I've lots to do."

The smile on Mr. O'Dwyer's face faded a little. He wondered when a man would come along who deserved the attention of a rare woman such as Sondra. Her bright smile and affectionate character served her well in hiding her secrets, but surely there was someone.

Sondra kissed his pale, thin cheek, handed the dog back to his owner with a smile, and continued on her way.

She would close her shop early today. A slumber party at Darcie's home was planned to celebrate. It wasn't the hen party that Sondra would have planned, but it was what Darcie wanted. Darcie wasn't one for crowds, and since she was newly pregnant, they figured a night in would be best. Sondra could make anything fun, and the two women always laughed together. So, it would be a fun night of junk food, gossip, and games, followed by an early afternoon wedding. Sondra looked up at the clear blue sky. It promised to be a beautiful weekend. And if there were a god up in Heaven, he would make sure that it was. If he didn't, then he would have to answer to her. Nobody deserved a beautiful wedding more than Darcie.

Sondra began to think about the past week's troubling events and shook her head. Those dark days were done. Now was the time to look to the future. She took a deep breath of the fresh morning air to clear away the terrible memories and continued on her way home.

Damn. The chubby postman with a comb-over who

suffered from halitosis was just ahead. He called her irritating, disgusting pet names like babe, tootsie, doll face, and her personal favorite: Split-tail. The very thought of his voice set her teeth on edge. Every time his eyes slithered up and down her body and he belched out one of those names, she wanted to cram her junk mail straight up his nose and stuff his chubby, red-cheeked face through her letterbox. Too bad there was nowhere for her to hide. He had already spotted her and waved. With a roll of her eyes, she met him at the end of her driveway, keeping him at more than arm's-length. But this particular morning, he smelled like a cookie, had gotten a new haircut, and greeted her with a cheerful "Good morning to you."

What a transformation! He asked about her plans for the weekend; since he was acting like a civilized human being, she engaged in the conversation and told him about the wedding. As Sondra had never given him the time of day before, he leaped at his opportunity and asked her out for a drink.

She took the mail from his hand and studied him for a moment. He'd finally used a toothbrush, some nice cologne, and a pair of scissors. That was quite an improvement. And because she was starved for male attention, she said yes. The postman didn't hide his delight. He took her hand and kissed it—a tender gesture that she had always enjoyed, but rarely was given. When he winked at her, she nearly dove across and bit him. He would have liked that.

Instead, she flashed him a smile and turned for her door. Sondra was saved from her moment of insanity when he called after her. "See you tomorrow, Split-tail." She turned back and informed the postman that the only splitting he would receive from her was her splitting open his thick skull. His smile quickly faded, and taking the rather violent hint; he scurried off on his rounds.

Once inside her house, she laid down her mail and looked at herself in the mirror. *Split-tail indeed! I'd rather deep fat fry my face than go out with him! That eejit needs directions to get to a point!*

She was desperate alright—but relieved to know she was not yet that desperate.

Want the recipes from the book? Sign up here.
www.judemclean.com

ARSE OVER IRISH TEACUP
A ROM-COM

Pre-Order Now
Coming March 2024

Even walking disasters need love.

Clumsy, quirky, and utterly charming, Beth Spinner is a
human whirlwind of catastrophes. While she is no stranger
to embarrassing situations, getting publicly dumped at her
grandmother's funeral is a whole new kind of
embarrassment. Deciding she's had enough, Beth takes a
page from her favorite Irish romance novel and sets off to
find her real-life dashing hero.

With her well-worn book in hand and infectiously positive
attitude, Beth boards a flight heading to the wild shores of
Ireland. But her adventure is already off to a rocky start
when she is seated next to Aidan, a grumpy curmudgeon
who is none other than the author of her favorite Irish

romance. And he is the most seemingly unromantic man she has ever met.

Aidan Turner is in a slump. How can a romance author write when he doesn't believe in love anymore? It's no wonder his publisher rejected his recent book. And the last thing he needs is the wide-eyed, idealistic woman chatting beside him as a reminder. No matter how adorable she is.

After landing in Ireland and a series of mishaps (who knew you had to drive on the wrong side of the road?), it seems Beth's luck may finally be turning around. Especially when she sees Aidan again at a wedding and he offers to be her tour guide. She may be a walking disaster, but no one deserves a poor experience when visiting such a beautiful country.

As Beth sees the man beneath the gruff exterior, and Aidan experiences his world through her eyes, fiction and reality blur. Life may not play out like a romance novel, but sometimes, you're given the opportunity to re-write your own love story.

REVIEW ESCAPE

Leave a review or star rating and make my day! No matter how long or short makes no difference. It will be much appreciated by me and other readers.

Thanks very much!
Jude xx

**Join Jude's readers group, Whiskey & Chocolate!
Receive exclusive updates, offers and laughs.
https://rb.gy/siyrt**

Anne Malloy
AN O'BRIANS NOVELLA

Sometimes true love demands an impossible choice ...

1789, Anne Malloy is a young woman trapped in a loveless marriage to a man who is cruel on the best of days. Despite her circumstances, she finds solace in her love for Lord Michael Godwin, a man who brings joy and passion into her life. But she's unaware of the looming threat that's waiting in the shadows and when Anne discovers she's pregnant with Michael's child, she faces an impossible decision.

About the Author

Jude McLean, a lover of whiskey and chocolate, vividly depicts her passion for sensory experiences within the pages of her Irish romance novels. Known for her boisterous laughter, she assures her readers that they'll never be deprived of laughs, gasps, perhaps a tear or two, and a heartwarming smile.

Sign up for Jude's newsletter to receive insider updates, offers, and laughs.
www.judemclean.com

 facebook.com/readjudemclean

 instagram.com/readjudemclean

 bookbub.com/authors/jude-mclean

ALSO BY JUDE MCLEAN

The O'Brians Series:

Escape, Book One

Break Free, Book Two

United, Book Three

Anne Malloy, An O'Brians Novella

An O'Brian Bride For Christmas, An O'Brians Novella

Return, Book Four Coming Soon

Surrender, Book Five Coming Soon

Other Titles:

Arse Over Irish Teacup, Coming March 2024

Made in the USA
Columbia, SC
22 October 2024

44906802R00162